Susan Finlay

Arriviste

a romantic novel

FIVE LINES IN THE SAND

Published in Great Britain in 2007
by Five Lines in the Sand Press Ltd.

Printed in the United Kingdom
by Lightning Source UK Ltd.

All rights reserved.
© Susan Finlay, 2007

The right of Susan Finlay to be identified as the
author of this work has been asserted in accordance
with the Copyright, Designs and Patent Act 1988.

ISBN 978-0-9556242-0-9

To my parents.

'I shall have a cup of tea afterwards', said Miss Braid. 'Can I get you a drink, dear, before I go?'

'My dear, if you would. It's a night, perhaps, for Chartreuse?'

'Yellow or green?' said Miss Braid's voice from the darkness of a cupboard. 'I can hardly see which is which.'

'Then put out both, my dear, if you would . . . I shall be drinking to your success.'

'You're so considerate of me, Antonia.'

'I am a person', said Antonia, 'who all her life long has been unable to decide whether she prefers green or yellow Chartreuse.'

Brigid Brophy, *The Finishing Touch*

Part 1

Hackney Wick

Alice Grisham liked a slap. As caffeine affected her similarly, it proved central to the late and waking hour. Ideally her preferred stimulant would be dispensed baby pale with a hardened artery of cream and consumed while looking out The Window. Alice aspired to be a hedonist. John insisted that black was a connoisseur's choice. Both being up they overlooked this intrinsic discord however - she made a pot for two.

In return John moved some of the ashtrays about. Before, the entire worktop had been covered with unwashed crockery, but now only half was covered at double the height. Plates jammed into each other, lost bills and scrawled-on envelopes were recovered. They unearthed a packet of half-cooked economy burgers that he began to pick at idly.

Alice poured the coffee from John's Heals' cafetiére and sat down. In her lap was a book – a biography of Rimbaud – that she intended, one day, to read. A used condom and beans on toast snaked out from underneath the sofa in a snail's trail of spunk and sludge. Beside her John alternated between the pictures in *Perfect 10* and the articles in *Artforum*. One was a tasteful men's magazine where all the girls had pretty faces but kept their knickers on, the other provided an awareness of the international art scene.

They stayed that way for some time, quietly and comfortably, and understanding each other. Personal advancement wandered alongside an element of artistic cliché with belief as a defining characteristic. They sipped their coffee together. John picked occasionally at a burger. Francoise Hardy played unobtrusively in the background. A dripping tap. Perhaps, in a bit, Alice would read the same article in *Artforum* that John had just read, think of an opinion, and then she and John might discuss it over a second coffee. Perhaps they would stay that way, doing those things, for what was left of the day...

But then Chris emerged from the bathroom. Water dripped behind him, and a soiled towel was dropped on the floor. He looked at them disparagingly, picked-up the least cooked burger he could find, and then took a large bite.

'That's disgusting,' said Alice. 'You'll get food poisoning.'

Leaning in towards him she became engulfed in a perfumed cloud - he must have knocked the bottle over while dying his hair to look like the Mafia. He had once put his hand through a window to prove a point on philosophy and ended up in A&E. Dye on his palms and the scent of orange blossom. It was an open-plan warehouse conversion. There was no escape.

Chris pushed another bloody handful between his lips and out-did John.

'Meat gives you energy,' he said. He leaned in and, being energetic, tried to give John's arm a gentle clout. John saw it coming and ducked. He stepped to the side and crashed noisily against the worktop's splintered edge. Chris contented himself with a half-hearted kick at his shin, a further push, and John threw the burger box at him.

'I need meat for energy,' Chris reiterated, and with conviction.

He took a second raw mouthful, and this time it was spat out on the floor. John and Alice exchanged a look, and in return Chris grabbed Alice by the neck. Alice didn't react, but let him shake her. She pictured herself dead and mildly fashionable, and recalled that the dropped perfume bottle had contained Vivienne Westwood's *Libertine*...

Chris let go of Alice and scowled. He walked over to the record player and took off the Francoise Hardy record. He didn't put it back in its sleeve. Then he found the remote control and sat down on the couch. An image of Robert De Niro being hit repeatedly in the face flashed across the screen.

Time now slumped for the duration of the film. Chris continued to pick on and off at the plate of rotten beef. Uniform spheres of red and grey sat alongside already-chewed remnants. They had bought the twenty on-offer packets the day before, and then cooked them all at once for no other reason than boredom and a weird, budget gluttony. (Chris turned up the volume on *Raging Bull*.) Fag ash, stale beer and what looked like a fingernail. Yet they had begun with such good intentions. Upon moving in they had even gone so far as to try to build a bar and throw a party with a Prohibition theme. They had taken pictures of their friends drunk on gin sloshed into china cups, certain that this proved A Very Good Time. They had run towards the future in retro accessories, talking big, and eager for more of whatever there was... and yet somehow, in spite of all this, they appeared to have become stranded in a dark arctic January, 2003, only too aware that their ill-informed D.I.Y. would never reach fruition. Ashtrays and plates were stacked and moved purposelessly about until drink and bickering interfered. Things were broken and lost with tears before bedtime. The warehouse had grown to be a cold, dirty and sordid bubble - unfit for human habitation and delighting in outrage.

They were only kids.

John pointed out one of the girls in *Perfect 10* to Chris - a pretty blonde with her lips slightly parted, hard pink nipples and white lace panties. Panties was definitely the right word. Wasn't she lovely?

'What's the point if you can't see her cunt?'

Chris had barely glanced at the picture. Instead his gaze stayed firmly on De Niro. He picked at the raw meat between his teeth. He wiped his dirty hand on his dirty trousers, sighed, sneered, turned the volume up and down. John let the magazine drop onto the floor. He gave Chris a look that said he couldn't be bothered. He narrowed his eyes considerably and put a lot of effort into showing just how not bothered he was. Chris put a lot of effort into not noticing. Alice threw a piece of meat on the floor in an absent way. It landed in the beans. By the towel.

'That's a nice jumper,' said John after a while, and Chris was forced to agree.

And actually it *was* a nice jumper. Navy blue Pringle, ultra-soft cashmere. It looked good against her olive and cream paisley scarf, but only if the scarf was knotted at the side. Often the knot would work its way to the front which looked too deliberate. It was upsetting. Paisley, Pringle and an English Rose complexion. Radically conservative in inverted commas. Alice sighed - life was overwhelming - and turned away from *Raging Bull.*

'The jumper's nice because it makes your skin look nice. You've got nice skin,' Chris said, and smiled, and looked attractive.

'Thanks. Your shirt is aspirational, but it's okay.'

'It's because I'm classical looking,' he told her.

Chris opened the usual bottle of wine. He had got out a book from the library and showed it to Alice. It was mainly pictures - a bit like a magazine. Chris agreed with Alice about what pictures were good and what pictures were bad. They agreed that most of it was alright but that they could do better if they put their minds to it. They said a lot of things like this. They both liked pulling faces.

John, who did not, stood up to cook a pizza. He piled up all the things from the piled-up half of the table so that they now took up only a quarter. He wiped the exposed section but did not wash any of the piled-up things, some of which fell on the floor. An already tender slab of beef was then laid on the table, and he began to pound it further with the end of a rolling pin. He intended that one of the pizza toppings would be steak, an organic steak, now a thin blood sponge of potential energy. *Mean Streets* was playing on the video. Chris and Alice looked at the book and the video, and pointedly ignored John, the domesticated, fancy-pansy, gaylord bastard. John finished pounding and moved over to the sofa. He put the chopping board on his lap and began awkwardly slicing basil. He accepted a glass of un-offered red wine. He believed in inclusion. A pause. Another glass. Then a continuation.

Alice stuck with her coffee for the time being, which went better with her navy jumper. She showed John the book on art and put it in an appropriate context. She explained what they had decided was good, and what they had decided was bad, and why they were better. Alice believed context to be one of her strengths. It was one of the reasons why she was good with clothes. She believed that you should always ascertain the context of a situation, and then pick an outfit just slightly to the side of it. That way you stood out, but not too much. It worked the same way with art but one shouldn't necessarily admit to it.

John was confused with why they liked what they liked, and the way they were so definite about it. He looked at the book with a puzzled expression.

'Aren't you being a bit fascist?' he said.

Alice and Chris looked at each other, and then looked at the television. John returned to the pizza. *Mean Streets* flickered. Italian-American men loved and fought and died, and Alice felt so much for those men - fighting for nothing, alone against the sky.

Chris and John finished the first bottle of wine and opened the second. Alice chain-smoked their Marlboro Lights because she was not a smoker herself, and being young, being artists, their talk turned to beauty.

'Beauty is out-dated,' Chris stated flatly. He was against it. He was a conceptualist. 'Beauty is dead.'

'Beauty is making a resurgence,' said John.

He had read an article about it in a previous edition of *Artforum* and spoke with authority. Sometimes when John spoke Alice felt that he walked on water, but occasionally that he lacked depth. Alice, who hoped to make a fourth painting, having already made three that counted, hoped that the fourth painting would be beautiful. She wanted very much to believe in absolutes, but so far her education had produced only two conclusions. One: that art was serious. Two: that art looked more serious when reproduced in black and white. Beauty therefore, as art, was fairly serious and possibly monochrome. At such moments one turned to John, and hoped to see him stride out, dry footed, across the sea.

'Sincerely, John, and I do mean this most sincerely,' Chris made a fist and brought it up towards his heart. Let no one question his sincerity. It came from the streets. 'Sincerely, John, beauty has no place in art anymore. It's just not relevant to the here and now. It's just... just... well, dead.'

'But then what has?' said John. This concerned him. *Artforum* was his bible. Death was a big subject.

Alice believed so much in beauty, and wanted to believe so much more. She brought her hand up against her forehead and opened her mouth in the ecstasy of the misunderstood – *poor, poor Alice!* – then caught herself before they caught her, and quickly stopped.

'Beauty exists, admittedly; the air in your pockets and all that stuff, but art's something more. It's about being clever. Art's saying, "Yeah I'm the man," and stamping it on the world,' Chris said, laughing, and playing up to the dissatisfied supremacy his upbringing had afforded him.

Alice believed in beauty. Believed in goodness, and in truth. Believed in something more. Believed in l'amour fou, heavy symbolism, the power of an image.

'You're an urban poet.' John shook his head with a weary superiority and turned the volume up a notch. He wasn't convinced. It wasn't as if Chris had ever written for *Artforum*. Or any publication. John had. He'd had a five-hundred-word review in *Contemporary Visual Arts* eighteen months ago. And been paid. Not much admittedly, but it was a question of principle.

'I believe in beauty,' said Alice.

She had dark hair with a heavy fringe. She had been termed an existential thinker by an internet personality quiz, but no one heard her. Instead they watched Harvey Keitel glide through a nightclub, while a black woman danced. Her nipple-tasselled breasts jiggled provocatively (it would have been hard for them to jiggle any other way), and her pants were probably panties. Harvey Keitel's character would later reveal concerns about being attracted to a black woman.

Alice turned the volume down with a caffeine trembling hand.

'I believe in beauty. Within an art context it can be transcendental.'

The words were picked out carefully, and she felt they were building towards a profound moment where they could all be saved. All she needed to do was abolish the sky and shine a torch into their darkness - give them a reason to believe and a shining light to head for. Alice sat a little straighter and blew a perfect smoke ring. A woman in the company of men. Context was strength:

'I just want to think that, and think that art matters and that it matters and that – ' and yet she was already faltering, jittery and unsure of the original point. But then she *had* sold three paintings. Someone had liked three of her paintings enough to buy them and hang them on a wall and see them every day. She would make a fourth. She must hang on to that. Then with conviction:

'Something matters that's all and that – '

'Oh Alice shut up,' Chris was predictable and irritated, 'I'll tell you what would matter. It'd matter if I fucked you up your arse. Alright?'

She felt unfairly thrown. How could he say something like that? How could he not be more aware and say something like that? Did he think that sort of thing was shocking? Did he think *The Shockingly Schlock Tactics of a Would-Be Angry Man* were shocking? She poured herself some wine and stared sullenly at her book. Chris folded his arms and sulked. John re-wound a missed section of *Mean Streets*, and this time it was he who sighed. Consistency continued. They could fight like kids on borrowed money, wasting time, while Hackney Wick kept life at bay.

'I'm fed up of Scorsese. Can't we watch something else?' asked Alice, who was suddenly always fed up with Scorsese.

'*Apocalypse Now*?' suggested John, who was particularly fond of the scene where bombs are dropped to classical music.

'*Full Metal Jacket*?' said Chris whose mood often changed abruptly, and was now enthusiastic again. 'Or another film about Nam?'

American men fighting for nothing, alone in the jungle. All the wives and sisters and mothers crying, forgotten, at home. Alice wasn't in the mood for Vietnam. What about Scrabble? That was a nice game that no one would agree to. What about Monopoly? It would be nice for friends to play games together of an evening. Or they could put Francoise Hardy back on, or talk sensibly about beauty, or do something, anything, other than stare into the boxed and flickering abyss.

John put on *Apocalypse Now* and Chris looked on approvingly.

Bang! Bang! He shot me down.

Then the continuation of boredom. It was a day like many.

The Wallace Collection

It had been six months since they had left art school. Six months since graduation. Since selling three paintings. Since top of the class, teacher's pet, the crème de la crème. Six months to look from the window of their ivory tower and suspect that experience could reach beyond the aesthetic. It was still only a suspicion, a dim ugliness that crept into an empty place, but it was there now and growing towards the real. And during those six long months of summer's end, which passed on through autumn's photogenic melancholy and into winter's icy heart, Alice Grisham, despite best intentions and firm beliefs, had failed to get a proper job.

In some ways this was awkward because Alice liked the look of money. Enjoyed knowing her lipstick was Yves Saint Laurent, seeing it mark the wine glass of expensive wine that tasted all the better for the knowing. Enjoyed buying into the shiny, gold make-up packaging. Enjoyed the seduction of artifice, the glossy sheen of commodity and despair. And money was a necessity for the very little luxuries of the day to day. For coffee, for museum shops, travel-cards, postcards, exhibition catalogues. She had sold three paintings after all. For entrance fees, cinema tickets, gallery talks. For her work. As an artist. She had sold three paintings. She hoped, one day, to make a fourth. Would make a fourth. And all these things were necessary for it. For experience and a necessary awareness. Money for books, for theories even. How could she think without a little money? A little sugar?

A little sweetness - *please.*

But credit cards could only go so far, and ultimately laziness would always compromise desire. *I might be shallow*, thinks Alice, *but I'm not committed.* She walks routinely alone, alongside the geriatric and dispossessed of weekday afternoons, fearful of change. She reads books in gallery cafes, asks for free perfume samples in large department stores, tries on designer dresses, visits museums...

And so today on a Sunday, which was much like a Monday, a Tuesday, and so on, Alice was stood in the Wallace Collection:

Her initial impression was always the same - that there was a great deal of gold. A molten heavy accent which, through a combination of occasional tables, ornamental cornices and scrolling picture frames, kept one in the dazzle of an ancient glint - this was the first layer. Second came the subtler, violet tints of Boucher's painted flesh and the soft, dove-greys of his wigs. Then the black marble cherubs that clung to a carriage clock. Then the pictures of doe-eyed slave girls who smiled out from under a sky coloured English blue. And it was always at this point, when the lure of gilt-edged exoticism was at its greatest, that the staircase swept her upstairs and climaxed in the fondant-coloured, satin-backed bit that she liked best – *Marie-Antoinette's very own furniture!*

Oh! The delicate delight at seeing the woman's Sevres' porcelain, of the tiny plates and cups made *just for her* – a girl married at fourteen, queen but a few years later, and then beheaded for treason at a mere thirty-seven years of age. It seemed fated in some way for someone who squandered a fortune on diamonds and sugar-craft while the populace starved. Who didn't understand the value of money or the cost of a thing, drank from an exquisite, miniature tea-set, and knew so much so young that would terrify a mother...

Alice stepped purposefully into the gift-shop. The comfortable scale of the postcards, the piped music (violins then harpsichord) the reproduction plates, would all, she felt, aid a tender introduction to the grand emotion of the grand interior, and all that this illicit, flushed cheeked, afternoon affair, entailed.

It was easier to have feelings in a period setting.

Camilla was looking out the window at the top of the stairs, one hand resting gently on the windowsill, one foot turned out a fraction to the left. It was a considered profile. She wore a white dress by Cacharel, white Aquascutum mac and white leather gloves from Topshop. Alice couldn't place the shoes, but they were white also. Camilla looked clean and committed to money.

They kissed and complimented, it went the same on every occasional Sunday, and arm in considered arm approached the tearoom. Camilla ordered a peppermint tea, which came in a white china pot, with matching white cups and saucers. Alice ordered a peppermint tea also. They contemplated scones, dieting being a suburban preoccupation, but decided against it, fat being cardinal. Camilla was wearing the new Marc Jacobs scent, which Alice had tried on only days before. Camilla had just bought two postcards and a notebook with a fan on it. Alice had nearly bought the same notebook and often bought postcards.

They sat against a coral pink backdrop, complete with potted palms, and discussed books. Camilla was reading *One Hundred and Twenty Days Of Sodom*, Alice was still on Rimbaud. They discussed who they'd seen since college. What they had found out about them. Who they still liked and whether or not they should swap books. Their conversations had a pace to them, known but not yet worn out, and the enjoyment of existing outside of Hackney Wick. Camilla, who smelt lightly of jasmine, was keen to exchange views on books. She was clever, it was flattering, but Alice's mind wandered.

'I feel bitter when I hear about people more successful than myself,' said Alice, without expecting a reply, and watched a fat woman with two scones at the next table. Both scones were heaped heavy with clotted cream. They looked small against her fat fingers, and white against her red hands. It disgusted Alice who was so easily disgusted. Camilla looked briefly at the woman and twitched her nose in an expression of amused contempt. Then she looked back at Alice. Camilla understood how Alice felt, and nodded and twitched to indicate this, but having lately become successful, having always been so very thin, it was literature that interested her now.

'Would you like to go out with the Marquis de Sade?' she asked.

'Oh no. Well, maybe. Well, just for a drink. Why, would you?'

'Oh no. He might shit in your mouth.'

(He might shit in your cunt.)

A comfortable silence followed.

The fat woman was really going for it with the scones. Little bits of cream and jam clung to the corners of her shiny mouth. A blob of jam snaked its way down her chin and into the clammy fold of an ageing neck while she sprayed the tablecloth with the froth of loose-gummed chewing. Alice and Camilla watched calmly while they sipped their tea. Some time elapsed.

'I would quite like a scone,' said Alice.

'Yes,' said Camilla. She swallowed the last of her tea and did not order a scone. Alice did the same, and a warm and bitter taste coursed down her throat and quelled her hunger.

Again they linked arms and walked round the collection. They both liked

French Romanticism, old money, weighty upholstery and the scent of polish. The mismatched, mercenary wishes of idealistic girls united and overwhelmed them. The curtains matched the wallpaper matched the cushions. The shoes matched the gloves matched the bag. There was closeness, but sometimes, unavoidably, the distance of different lives, fears that were understood but no longer shared. But then it was so nice to have a friend. One who might buy a notebook with a fan on it, the same notebook that you might like to buy!

'That's a good blouse' said Camilla. It was a good blouse, floral print Paul and Joe with pussy-bow detail. It seemed a little bleached out now, in the considered context of the white and the gold, by the blinding tyranny of taste.

Camilla had recently moved in with her boyfriend, an older man, and also neat. Their flat was immaculate with views, minimal furnishings in neutral tones and up-lighting. Underneath the sink were industrial cleaning products and thick black eraser-gloves like a murderer might have. It was a life far beyond Alice. Alice of listable aspirations and looked-after belongings. A world far beyond the Wallace Collection whose accessibility came as a result of belonging to no one...

Alice thought about money and felt a mixture of respect and uncertainty. It played on her mind in a bourgeois manner. She touched the bow at her neck and tried to concentrate on what Camilla was saying:

Camilla was going to have a small party in a month or so, or an exclusive gathering, as she called it. Camilla valued exclusivity. She didn't spread herself too thinly, and gave her all to the privileged few, twitched and nodded at outsiders, and then carried on with enviable certainty. She gave a typically subtle shoulder-shrug, and said that it might be nice to serve White Russians. Maybe also to have some sort of Constructivist-type painting as decoration – there was an old calendar that could be cut into squares – because the party would have a Russian theme. Camilla was into Russia, the coldness and cruelty as a picture-book style - Venus in all her furs aboard the Trans-

Siberian Express and Julie Christie weeping in *Dr Zhivago*. Black swans, white snow, sable hats, vodka and embroidery. A picture-book with woodcut illustrations, printed in jewel coloured inks on thick, thick parchment, bound in leather, and kept inside a box.

Alice also liked Russia, but on the whole her tastes were more European and ideally some gold would be involved. Whatever the theme was however, it would be excessive. Camilla worked in a commercial art gallery now, and life had quickened its step.

'They threw a terrible party recently,' said Camilla, referring to her employers, 'honestly, terrible, wrong even - with a dog. A dog, Alice, for doing terrible things with. It was in South Kensington. In a Georgian mansion with a marquee in the garden – that's the bit where everything was going wrong with the dog – and there were crates and crates of Cristal and beautiful white flower arrangements everywhere but...' there was a second's pause as distaste flickered quick across small features, 'but anyway, enough of that, bring the boys. Bring John and Chris.'

'Oh yes, of course.'

'Oh, and of course Rory.'

Sometimes Alice slept with Rory Brown, a man of infinite politeness, in an effort at normality. Like the dog, she preferred not to dwell on it.

'Yes, maybe.'

'Oh well, fine then.'

The look was needlessly sharp. Rory had been Camilla's friend initially. Camilla understood but did not approve. Occasionally she would spit out a tiny nastiness, and then call it being honest. Briefly arms dropped to their sides. Occasionally Alice felt a huge and out of scale surge of irritation and made sure she let it show. They walked on in silence at an avoidable distance until mutual enthusiasm for a light fitting brought them together once more.

Alice's gaze followed Camilla's gloved hand and looked upwards. A chandelier hung from the mouth of a golden sun. The walls were daffodil yellow silk, still bright in the subdued lighting. Out of time. Alice closed her eyes and felt the warm colour press against the shut lids, delirious. Were there modern equivalents to this? To this all-consuming gigi-ness? This joy in the pointless? Of course there were. A thousand and one fashionable delights to decorate an already busy world, and to most of which she was susceptible. Next birthday someone could get her a World of Interiors subscription. To press a pink cheek against a golden sun. Have you ever been to paradise?

'Have you ever been to the Opera?' asked Alice, 'I've never been.'

They had known each other a long time and Camilla didn't answer. She was caught up in the light. They both stared up at the sun, and hot little spots of yellow danced over their vision. They looked at the wallpaper and the things in cabinets. Camilla took off her gloves and gingerly touched the yellow silk. Alice looked out the window, where a wintry London night was framed brightly. It was a lovely moment, and then finished.

Arm in arm they returned to the gift shop. Examined the porcelain plates reproduced on tin. Alice rapped her knuckles on one, and made a noise.

'Victorian working class,' she said, and the warmth of providing a context flooded over her. She caught her reflection in the gift shop mirror, large and edged in gold. Her skin glowed the way it does in stately homes. The lighting was soft, the mirrored glass old and backed in green. It was the treatment to the back of the glass that determined whether or not a mirror was flattering. It was more than just the light or how well you were feeling. Camilla agreed about the plates. They would be just the thing for a sophisticated picnic. By sophisticated she meant classy. But she was sophisticated. Camilla bought an exclusive set of six. They decided to walk around the Wallace Collection for a third time, and sometimes they linked arms.

They came upon a Fragonard:

       An eighteenth century girl
       In eighteenth century petticoats
       Swings on a swing on the branch of an apple tree.
          And all around her leaves–
          A framed oblong of eerie bluish foliage–
          Become the swirling sky of a storm.
              But she, oblivious to background
              Just soars higher! Higher! Higher!-

                          Oh! The joy! Of vice!

       The Second Man holds the rope
       Pulls hard back on it
       And digs in his heels.
          Stone Cherubs look-on in the silent manner of the ancients
          Raise their eyebrows in the camp style of the modern.
              Dark clouds continue to gather.

       But her gaze is fixed on The First.
          One white, stockinged leg reached out towards him
          One silk slipper kicked off in reckless abandon.

       And he falls willingly.
          Is buoyed up by the shrubbery.
              Looks past the froth of her skirts –
                  And soars higher still!

    'They didn't wear knickers then so it would have been very rude,' said Alice as the context changed. They looked at *The Swing* for a bit. It passed. They moved on.

    The next room contained glass cabinets of nude miniatures. Curtains of green leather protected them from direct light. A card instructed that they lift them up to view the works, and Alice obliged for a further glimpse of the erotic. The women depicted were rotund looking, smiley sorts with slappable bottoms, rosy cheeked and arsed and much in-keeping with the Fragonard look.

'It should say part flaps,' said Camilla with a lapse in sophistication, pointing at the card.

Well there might just be time for one more pot of peppermint tea before home. Camilla would treat Alice as she was better off. No, no, she would like to, why would she say it if she didn't mean it? They walked back to the tearoom, sat down and breathed out. Camilla draped her coat over her lap - fabrics blurred - it was too perfect a juxtaposition. Alice brushed a piece of lint from her sleeve and touched the bow at her neck. So well dressed and secure was the company of women, so soft and well lit.

A handbag was placed on the table as Camilla searched inside for a lighter. It was a gorgeous white, cream and camel snakeskin clutch with a pearl clasp. *All different types of snakes*, thought Alice admiringly. She watched as Camilla rummaged, found and then lit a Vogue menthol, extra-slim white-filter cigarette. Alice had a cigarette too. Her burgundy nail polish was as yet un-chipped, smooth and seductive against the snow-white filter tip. They contemplated a crème-brûlèe, but ultimately decided against it.

Alice handed Camilla one of the earpieces on her walkman. She wanted Camilla to hear the new Goldfrapp song.

'I've only just got this,' said Alice, who liked to keep track of things, 'the cover's really good, a nice typeface,' (she liked typefaces, a commercial admission) 'and there's a wolf, and she's wearing red shoes. I only ever listen to a couple of the songs.'

'I've got the new Moloko. In places it's quite stylish. I feel stylish when I put it on,' said Camilla by way of a response. She was also aware when it came to typefaces.

'Lara did a photo shoot with Roisin Murphy. She doesn't have a stylist or anything,' said Alice. Lara was one of their friends in fashion. She worked on a magazine and socialised with the semi-famous.

'Really? Does Alison Goldfrapp have a stylist?'

'Yes, she has a stylist.'

'She must have a good stylist. She looks too good. She doesn't look styled.'

'Yes. They must be a good stylist.'

Alice liked listening to women's voices, especially when they sang of love and loss. There should always be a woman, preferably a soul-singer, to sing of this. To sing of it continually. A great stylist and a heart that would not mend.

And as is the nature of revelation, it seemed that a break from the lethargy was possible. *Underneath the paving stones the beach!* A great stylist, a great red jumper and a great Joan of Arc bob, a pleated skirt to grace the knee, and a coat with the collar turned up. She thought of Chris's library book from the other night. It had contained high contrast black and white photographs of well-dressed students protesting in the Paris of 1968. They wrote poetic slogans and read philosophy, embraced the moment with pictorial and charismatic intelligence. In one, the best one, Alice's favourite, a particularly pretty idealistic pupil in a plaid dress stood at the front, a metaphorical lamp held high above her head, a light shining bright into the darkness with the passion of ideas not yet disproved or disparaged. Shining bright with belief! Alice thought then, as now, that she had missed her calling, been born too late. She spoke reasonable French, read poetry, drank coffee on her own and felt misunderstood. One looked inwards, felt soft, felt sad. She had a beret but somehow this was less than enough.

'Did you say whether or not you'd ever been to the Opera?' asked Alice, with a slight but deliberate shift of focus.

Camilla was concentrating on her cigarette. She was still annoyed about the stylist. It was apparent in the way she flicked the ash.

'No I haven't,' she said finally, 'but I had afternoon tea at Covent Garden once. Crispin,' (that was Camilla's boyfriend) 'says they're doing *La Traviata* there this summer.'

'And what happens in that?'

'Violetta dies for love of Alfredo.'

Alice's wine glass trembled in her fragile hands - hands that longed to wipe away a crystal tear. Love and death, and death and love. She would swoon and if she couldn't swoon then she would die. The Opera sounded fabulous.

Camilla was less concerned with the Opera.

'Well, who's her stylist?' she said.

'I don't know. I think Lara knows.'

Lara was the trendy friend. Camilla was the sophisticated friend. And Alice sat midway, the intersection in a Venn diagram of preference, and thought about the opera, scones, and crème-brûlèe.

They had another peppermint tea and re-examined the notebook with a fan on it. They discussed the ingredients needed for a White Russian. They talked about their friend Armond, who had recently been to hospital. They talked about many things that they liked, and dissected some that they did not. Alice thought about typefaces. It was so nice to have girls as friends. It was civilised.

Hackney Wick II

Chris and Alice were trying to organise an exhibition. This happened every month or so. Then the pressures of communal living built to a breaking point. Then postponement. Then grief for loss. Then the cycle would begin again, rising and falling at the exact same third-year art school level as when it first began. Consequently Alice sometimes ran into people who already knew of the exhibition and wanted to know more. If it was ever going to happen, for instance. Her replies swung between the vague or the more vague, depending on the state of Chris and herself, and secretly a sense of annoyance that they dared to question such a thing.

Having remained on good terms for two weeks, having become exceptionally fed-up, the subject raised its tenacious head. Alice felt feeble.

'There's been too much hype. We have to keep it very low key. Let's just throw a massive party and then slip in the art in like an afterthought.'

'I don't want my work presented as an afterthought,' said Chris.

'I know, I know, but it's the only way we can survive it now.'

'When you say that Alice, I feel as though you don't care, and I find that upsetting.'

He allowed his bottom lip to almost tremble - sometimes he could be sly. He didn't find it upsetting. He found it annoying. If they were going to plan an exhibition together then he needed Alice to have faith in his grand vision. Then organise it for him in practical terms. He had been in a show shortly after leaving college that had been indisputably clever. But no one had really seen it or written it up, ('It's not like I care', he said, and too often). This time he would structure it differently. This time, was time to take something back. Chris ran his hands through his hair with genuine agitation. He would probably have a break-down before he was thirty.

In contrast Alice fell back on a patch of never-hoovered carpet - effete. She watched a spider crawl across the ceiling with what looked like an egg sac on its back. It was one of the days when they didn't leave the warehouse and endlessly went on, with life and at each other. The exhibition demanded completion of the fourth painting, and she felt it might go better if presented as a joke.

'I don't want to be in an exhibition that's anything less than the best. I want to show all those talentless fuckers that get in *Time-Out*,' Chris said. He had drawn a serpent on his forearm in biro and his left leg twitched in time to Iggy Pop.

'Well that's how I feel too,' said Alice. It was how she felt. It was how they both felt. It was the principal set back to the Great Exhibition of 2003. 'Did I tell you I saw Nicki and Sam at the Tate?'

Nicki and Sam were two people from their year at college, whose not-so-unique brand of contrived irritation had since proved commercially viable.

'That's exactly the sort of thing we're up against!'

He put down the biro in the grip of a disturbed instant. *Nicki and Sam.*

Nicki and Sam. Talentless fucks. He'd show them. It rose angrily above them like a crime scene helicopter. The thought might send him insane. It circled them both, an angry buzzing of discontent, buzzing and droning that others were getting ahead, droning and buzzing with fidgety disquiet.

'I don't think we should think about Nicki and Sam,' said Alice, failure being a terrifying prospect, 'it's not a competition.'

'You brought it up!'

'It was playing on my mind!'

'Now it's playing on *my* mind!'

Nicki and Sam. Nicki and Sam. And on and on and on ad infinitum.

Chris and Alice were fed-up. They might plan an exhibition and it terrified them. Hysteria rose and levelled. Chris allowed his lip to almost tremble again, he expected too much, and Alice stared blankly, niggardly, back at him. They had come to a familiar standpoint.

'Would you like a coffee?' said Alice.

She got up and put her shoes back on (this was important when navigating the sticky grit of the warehouse floor) and went to put the kettle on. While she was waiting for it to boil she washed up some mugs. Not just the two mugs that they needed, but all the mugs in the sink. She measured out the coffee in the cafetiére. Then she re-sealed the bag and put it back in the fridge. She found a half-eaten packet of Jammy Dodgers and put them on a plate on a tray. Then, when the kettle had boiled and the water been poured into the cafetiére, she put it back on the tray along with the full fat milk and a packet of brown sugar, which she always bought because she preferred it. She carried the tray back over to where Chris was sitting. He pushed several biscuits in his mouth at once.

'You'd make a good wife,' he said, between the crumbs. It was a horrible thing to say. They both smirked apathetically. Alice began flicking through Italian Vogue. Some of the things were really good - big hair and red lips, old-fashioned hats with veils. Without realising she ate four Jammy

Dodgers.

'You ought to watch yourself,' said Chris, watching Alice, 'that's what bored women do. They turn to the fridge.'

'If we're going to do an exhibition,' said Alice, putting down her biscuit, 'then it ought to have a theme. I don't think we should be afraid of having a *fashionable* theme – '

'I'm not interested in beauty. I've told you. It's dead,' said Chris, who had seen it coming. 'I think we need to do something that's controversial and aggressive.'

Controversial *and* aggressive. This was easier said than done. It was another of the exhibition's setbacks. Chris returned to the Jammy Dodgers. He added biro scales to the snake, and then rubbed them out again with a spitty finger. Controversial *and* aggressive. Alice admired his consistency.

'This is my favourite Iggy Pop song,' he said, eating more biscuits. They were listening to *Some Weird Sin*.

Alice sat up off the floor and removed a piece of fluff from her Jonathan Aston seamed stockings. She thought about the stockings and whether or not she had nice legs. The song finished and then silence. Soon all the biscuits were gone. Chris had had eleven and Alice had had three and a half. He was considerably bigger than she was, but not to that ratio.

'What will this controversial and aggressive exhibition consist of?' she asked. 'My next painting, your next photographs, and...?'

'It'll be futuristic.'

'Futuristic?'

'Yes.'

A Blue Peter image of tin foil and coat hangers stuck in her head. *I am too literal,* she thought, (*and old fashioned*). She stood up off the floor and snagged a heel. A ladder sped to her thigh, and fifteen pounds worth of elegance was ruined in a lightening flash. There was a second's annoyance where the exhibition faded into pointlessness beside the laddered stockings.

'Why don't we have a Futur*ist* theme?' said Alice. She thought it was an art movement that might appeal to men. 'The Futurists were great. They were into industry and machines and the concept of speed. Mainly the concept of speed. They were Italian. Their British rivals were the Vorticists, who preferred to champion the concept of the vortex. We could go with speed, or the vortex.' She was speaking as though to a child, one she could rescue through superior knowledge, and happily she raced towards her conclusion. 'We can have a glamorous Italian style party afterwards, and everyone can have big hair and red lips!'

'The Futurists are not futuristic as they are nearly ninety years old and therefore now out of date. And anyway stop being so literal,' said Chris.

Bang! Bang!

The stockings were ruined. Her legs were alright. Chris had found a packet of felt-tips and began to colour-in the serpent's head a lurid purple. Sometimes when it reached this point it was best to just ignore everything and keep on going.

'I went to a good party with a Hitchcock theme,' said Alice, 'Hitchcocktails. Every one had red lips and *blonde*, though sometimes big, hair, like one of his heroines. Wigs you know. One man went as a shadow which I thought was clever. There was a wheel that you could spin to determine the manner of his bitter end. I was amazed by the style – '

'We're planning an art exhibition not a party. You never take this seriously,' broke in Chris. A giant purple serpent now ran from wrist to shoulder, in places shakily.

'I don't see the difference,' said Alice, who took it very seriously indeed.

Mess and blood poisoning.

Alice put the pens back in their packet and placed them on a high shelf. Chris scowled.

'Would you like another coffee?' she said.

'If you like.'

Alice put her shoes back on, put all the things back on the tray, and then carried it back over to the sink. She filled up the kettle and rinsed away the old coffee dregs from inside the cafetiére. She thought about the smell of coffee being nicer than the actual taste, but decided that observations on promise and fulfilment were not worth sharing when they lay on the domestic plain. One would rather think about Hitchcocktails. Red lips and the fashion of fascism. She wiped away the spilled coffee and rinsed out the mugs. Then when the kettle had boiled, everything was carried back over again.

'You've made it too strong. Last time you got it right but this time it's too strong,' said Chris, and sipped and winced. He spilt some coffee on the floor but didn't bother to do anything about it.

Alice opened up Italian Vogue again. There were some good hats. Tiny islands of glut, of feathers, fruits and birds. Stern arcs of straw and then sudden bursts of feathers, fruit and birds - grace notes on a modernist composition. Fashion was so clever because it always took a side. Fashion was an incitement to violence. Red lips, black net and feathers - an image like that gave you something to aim for. Alice offered Chris the magazine:

'Do you prefer the ones with the feathers or the ones with fruit or the ones with birds?'

'Feathers.'

'Why feathers?'

'The feathers are real feathers. The birds and fruit are imitation.'

It had never occurred to Alice to judge a hat on those terms, only which was prettier and which was trendier. Maybe Chris' view was radical. Maybe Chris' view was more conceptual, or maybe it was more dated. Like Chris it sat firmly on the fence, a step from possible greatness, a step from emotional agoraphobia, until it finally became something and forced a response.

'What's wrong with imitation? In the context of a hat?'

'I don't know. It's just creepy.'

'Couldn't you fancy a girl in a hat?'

'No'

'Bet you'd sleep with one though, if the offer presented itself.'

'Probably.'

Chris slept with a lot of girls. The standard varied, but he was a conceptualist. Alice looked at the hats with a new sense of perspective. They still looked good to her. She'd still wear one - one with fruit and birds and feathers.

'Maybe Futurism could be controversial *and* aggressive,' said Chris. He was capable of kindness, especially when he suspected his audience's interest of waning.

The prettiest, trendiest hat was actually just net and feathers. A very young, red-haired model wore it tilted over one eye. She was the prettiest, trendiest model. Her full lips were painted so dark red they were nearly black. One finger pulled at the lower lip, her nails were the same shade also. Her skin was freckled marble, hazed through a veil. She looked into the middle distance with kohl rimmed, half-shut eyes. The hat gave her an edge, a grace note on beauty. Futurism faded as Alice thought about hats.

Coffee

For want of somewhere better to go she was stood in the Liverpool Street Starbucks, clutching a notebook to her chest and fumbling with several different pens. The atmosphere was an invasive one of sour testosterone, where one man spoke too loudly about the possibility of virtual worlds, and his associate admired a new Tag watch, not listening. He turned his wrist in slow absorption so as to let the glass catch the light and, inadvertently, a small circle flitted across Alice's forehead. She placed her order - a tall mocha with extra cream - and blinked, mole like. She realised that she was also hungry and ordered a granola bar. Apparently this was the best breakfast substitute available from a coffee shop chain. Second was the skinny breakfast muffin. While waiting she sent several text messages to friends - a steady drizzle flecked down from the mackerel coloured sky - eventually her phone beeped back – C U L8R X. She added sugar to her coffee, blinking intermittently, contemplating the truncated nature of modern communications.

The men beside her moved on from being cyber nerds and began talking about someone at the office who annoyed them. Their reasons seemed arbitrary. They collected their drinks and sat down. The one with the Tag took his jacket off and laid it over the chair arm. He was nearly good-looking and force of habit made Alice look to see what the label was. It said Hugo Boss. She wasn't sure what view she held on Hugo Boss. Sometimes she thought he had a modern, sporty approach to design, but at other times that he was common. She had nearly bought a skirt in the Selfridges' winter sale, but something had held her back, something she had remembered about the firm being founded on money from the Nazis. Or then again, maybe just the fact that he was common.

The Tag man had deliberately placed the jacket over a magazine but Alice could still see most of it - a photograph of an Amazonian blonde with four cocks up her various holes. Four. It didn't look comfortable. The man caught her looking and reddened. He shifted his jacket so as to conceal the picture. He hunched away from her and towards his colleague.

Alice thought about the various pornos that had gradually infiltrated the warehouse, and the way it annoyed her when she remembered to be annoyed by it. She decides that when she gets home she will collect them all up, together with the Roy 'Chubby' Brown video and the complete writings of Donald Judd, and tape them secure and disapprovingly inside a cardboard box. This box can then be hidden behind the sofa under the guise of 'having a tidy', and left to slowly gather grime. Alice sanctioned herself a small, deviant smile at a small, deviant plan, sipped her coffee, and thought about jobs:

'Escort'. She wrote it in orange felt-tip at the top of her note pad. Orange was a positive colour associated with Buddhism. That was why Buddhists wore orange. (Like most students she had flirted with alternative religion, but being an aesthete it had been short-lived. After a while she had found Schopenhauer and preferred to let things slide from there.) She thought about being an escort and concluded that it wouldn't actually be too hard. That one good quality black dress, a knowledge of wine and which fork to use, or maybe even just smiling would be enough.

'Actress.' She wrote it in a baby-pink pen, but then she didn't know where to begin with that one. She sickened slightly with distaste. And crossed it out again.

'Waitress.' Now that was stooping very low. That was demeaning. She couldn't do it, not now that she was no longer suburban and thought that if you weren't rich you had to act like you weren't. Low pay and hours that dragged. People couldn't live like that. It wasn't right. Alice crumpled up the piece of paper and put it in the bin. Then she looked at the fresh piece of paper, ready to begin again. There followed a long and considered mental pause.

There was a blue felt-tip. Blue was an intellectual colour. Or so she had read. 'Gallerist.' 'Magazine Editor.' Written in a large and cursive script. But these fell into the impossible. She may as well have written 'Artist.' Another pause. 'Cinema Usherette?' It had a kind of low-level glamour. Alice put the lid back on the blue felt-tip. Or a 'Window Dresser', now that might be fun. The coffee was too sweet. Maybe she should go and see a film instead.

Some people say they feel old when they feel sad, young when they feel happy. Alice put the top back on a blue felt-tip and felt neither. *I exist*, thought Alice, and a hand snatched despairingly at the ether. *I am a site for existence.* Ultimately, always, aware, cursed by a small degree of insight and consequently lacking in confidence, Alice sits in silence and feels low. She gets out all the felt-tip pens and rearranges them in rainbow order. She thinks about whether the rescuee can ever be the rescuer. Whether a woman who looks out the window can ever be relied upon, or if a man who claims to feel old can ever be trusted. Alice puts the pens back in her bag. She sips her coffee and twists a loose strand of hair too tight around her index finger. Her phone beeps. She ignores it. Alice thinks about being an Escort. It often ends up this way.

The businessman puts his jacket back on. It is a bad cut and colour on him and prevents him from being attractive. The magazine is shoved haphazardly inside a leather hold-all with further crimsoned furtive gesturing. He has the stooped posture of an office drone coupled with the acerbic zest of an undesirable man. 'Chairman of the Board.' 'Chief of Police.' It would be written in red. Alice's approach to existence is elitist:

She will never wear Hugo Boss.

'Gallery Assistant.' 'Magazine Intern.' Like John, who works at an art magazine and was once paid hard cash for a five hundred word review. His well-shod foot on the first rung of a ladder he might actually want to climb. *I might go and see a film* thinks Alice. *I might buy another coffee. Sleep with a murderer, go to Topshop, jump off a cliff...*

Inertia is deadening. It alters the scale of life, flattens out everything to the same monotonous level. Cinema Usherette – it was the last bastion of hope. *I might buy another coffee,* thinks Alice.

She buys another coffee and stays sat in the Liverpool Street Starbucks for want of somewhere better to go. It often ends up this way. She decides that what she would really like to do is to go abroad. To lie in the sun and feel the romantic distance of the language barrier, or else to walk across a snowy foreign landscape and be so deeply alive. To not communicate, to retain a little mystery, to exist within an out-of-context English Rose appeal - but how to begin? How to ever be brave enough to begin?

Alice sips her coffee and thinks about how much she might enjoy being a Cinema Usherette. She considers the darkness and insulation from the world necessary for desire. Perhaps there, in the velvet gloom, she would discover a place beyond representation. Discover a chamber that allowed for the experience of feelings. She sees a girl stood alone in the dark. She is holding a torch. Ambition ebbs and flows. And Alice sips her coffee.

Café Kick

'Kate Moss is a filthy bitch. She had two blokes on her, licking out coke from her arse-hole.' Lara pushed the hair out of her eyes. She was tired from a party she had been at the night before. It had been very cool. Kate Moss had been there. Lara's friend nodded. Yes, Kate Moss was supposedly a slag. His friend nodded too. They were all very excited about it.

His friend, who had also brought a friend, got up to buy a round. It was happy hour in Café Kick, a cafe-bar with a Brazilian football theme. There were lots of deliberately battered looking table-football tables and fake flowers and chilli pepper shaped fairy lights. Lara tied her hair back with a bobble. She was wearing a leopard print top that showed an impressive cleavage. She hadn't done this before. Alice supposed that she must always have had those tits, but that usually they'd stayed hidden under a jumper. Their discovery was proving to be a somewhat startling revelation. The three men were transfixed.

'It may even have been three blokes,' said Lara, transfixing with her previously concealed breasts. She was remaining non-committal as to whether or not she had witnessed the incident herself. She took her hair back out of the bobble and snorted the last white line of powder.

'Could it have been four?' asked Alice, unfazed by the story's lack of primary sources (and had Kate Moss been wearing a hat?). Lara thought hard, brushed her fringe to one side. Now she thought about it, it *could* have been four.

The friend of the friend, who was called Geoff, came back with the drinks. Lara had a large circle of ever changing friends. Sometimes Alice felt that they morphed into one giant blob of the officially cool people. A snowball of twisted levis and import trainers rolling downhill through Hoxton, growing bigger, gaining speed, blurring. Geoff had a pleasant, indistinct look about him. He was wearing green and white Adidas with green laces, a possibly ironic rugby shirt, and had just bought Alice a Mojito. This consisted of brown sugar, mint, soda, rum, lime juice and something she couldn't work out. It was very nice. She must tell Camilla about Mojitos, and Brazil, but she might forget, and besides, Camilla was more of an indoor girl, and Russia more sophisticated than Latin America. As a general rule Alice saw sophistication and levels of sweat as being closely linked. In Russia only the peasants sweated and everyone else looked good in fur. This was a fact.

Alice and Geoff began a polite conversation. Geoff was a Modern Creative like everyone else they knew. He used to work at the magazine where John now worked and knew John and some of the people that John knew. Geoff preferred the idea of Brazil to Russia because he liked to get a tan in summer and didn't sweat much. Alice conceded that it was nice to get a tan. Geoff had also been to the cool party.

'Kate Moss is pretty, isn't she?' said Alice, 'and small. I know all models are small but she's really small.'

One of the other men disputed that all models were small. He had met a girl at the cool party who had said that she was a model and who had been very voluptuous.

'She's not a model. She's just rich and wants to be a model and fucked the right person. The photographer who did that shoot didn't pick her until she insisted he do her in the arse. They were going at it in the toilets. He lubed himself up with Blistex 'cos they didn't have anything else and everyone outside could hear her squealing like a tortured piglet. She's not a model, just some B-list star-fucker with puppy fat,' concluded Lara. She bent in towards one of the men who lit her cigarette and then drew back, knowingly superior. She knew how things worked. Lara was attractive in a severe way and too short to be a model. She was wearing turquoise leggings and pink ankle boots that caused her to strut. Alice was wearing her drainpipe jeans and Pringle jumper because the drink was officially last minute and no big deal.

Geoff went away and came back with another Mojito. He said that he had just got a text message about a party later. It sounded good and he'd be going and they were all invited. Would Alice like to come along too?

Alice was in two minds about going because, in truth, she didn't like going back to Hackney Wick on her own late at night. The road was dark without proper lighting and one of their neighbours had recently been mugged at the station. Often there was a car on fire and once, strangely, a caravan.

'Why don't you move somewhere safer?' asked Geoff. He looked concerned. A woman shouldn't have to face a burning caravan late at night. Perhaps he was decent like John, whom he also knew. 'Why not move into Hackney Central, then there'd be more people around.'

'Because Hackney Wick makes me feel like I'm really living,' said Alice and took a gulp of Mojito. Everybody laughed.

'Alice lives in a fantastic warehouse conversion. It's the perfect party house. A while back they had a fantastic party with a prohibition theme,' said Lara, who had been impressed by Alice's white fur stole.

'A prohibition theme?' said Geoff.

'Only nothing was prohibited,' said Lara and laughed again and sharply and quickly added 'but I really liked Alice's outfit.'

Lara had gone home afterwards with some people none of them really knew and had never mentioned what had happened. Sometimes Lara got really trashed and did terrible things with several people all at once and then had to claim she'd blacked-out. It was part of her charm.

'What, nothing?' said Geoff. He raised an eyebrow. 'What did you get up to then?'

'Not a lot really,' said Alice.

'Oh come on.' He laughed in a jokey, knowing way, as a man in the company of women. And some other men. But aiming mainly at the women.

'No really, not a lot. I served gin in china cups. That was about it. Camilla's going to have a party soon though, one with a Russian theme.' Feeling that this was not enough, she went on to give a little more. 'In fact Camilla went to a terrible party recently. Everyone had to take off their clothes and wear pillow cases over their heads as soon as they arrived so no one knew who anyone was. In the garden was a huge marquee, and when they went inside there was a man shagging a dog. It was in South Kensington.'

'What type of dog?' asked one of the men.

'I don't know,' said Alice. 'I mean, a man made love to an animal. In public. Does the breed really matter?'

'Well it'd seem less grim if it was a big dog' said Geoff. 'A Yorkshire Terrier just wouldn't work.'

There was a nauseous hush as Geoff made five obscene syllables, invoking the frenzied yaps of a ridiculous, possibly dying, animal. Alice sipped the second Mojito. Lara pulled at her bra-strap until she thought of something else to say.

'Camilla's the perfect party hostess. She lives in a fantastically minimal flat with fantastic views,' she said finally, providing an unnecessary explanation and an upbeat note. The three men nodded. Geoff stroked the side of his face.

Alice sipped the second Mojito. The other two men got up to play table football. Lara said she'd play the winner and went to stand by the side. Alice turned so as to face Geoff more. It was too dark to look out the window.

'Where do you live then?' asked Alice. It seemed as good a thing to say as any other.

'Stoke Newington. It's great.'

'And what's that like then?'

'It's great. A really laidback kinda vibe.'

A really laidback kinda vibe? He must be a really laidback kinda guy. Perhaps he had a really great laidback kinda life.

'Sounds great,' said Alice and gave him her brightest, most interested smile. He was probably a nice, pleasant, decent man after all, and it was too dark to look out of the window. 'I like your trainers,' she added.

'Thanks, they're limited edition. I like your jumper.'

'Thanks, it's cashmere.'

Alice smiled at Geoff and Geoff smiled at Alice.

Over the other side of Café Kick Lara was playing the winner. She bent over the table football table showing both her cleavage and her arse so that every angle gave a view of at least one of these two assets trembling with spasms of laughter. Her eyes creased up into sooty slits of eyeliner, and her hair fell into her eyes. It wasn't egotism, just a style, and everyone loved Lara, who loved life and never refused. She would probably win at table football, then she could play Alice or Geoff. Then they could play each other. Geoff looked at Lara's arse then looked back at Alice.

'It must be easy to paint.'

'What?' The conversation had jumped on a stage without her realising.

'Living in a warehouse. Lots of room. It must be great not having to go to a studio and waste all that time travelling and moving stuff. Just get out of bed and get on with it. I bet you're really prolific.'

'Yes. Yes I am. I am working on a fourth painting. Yes. It's great.'

For some reason this sounded false. But she was working on a fourth painting. Or planning to. And yet when she had asked about the trainers which, not being much of a trainer person, she hadn't actually liked, it had sounded sincere. Alice wondered if she and Geoff were the same deep down, just fashion conscious and slightly awkward. And Geoff was keen to continue chatting. He had also studied painting at art-college, a few years ago now though, and seen it as a golden time.

'What sort of work are you into?' he said. 'I have to say, I have been known to dig some pretty crazy shit.'

Really? The hot Brazilian sun froze over and the world ended not in fire but in ice. Oh, really? Could such a laidback kinda guy dig shit with a crazy vibe? Really. He was so profoundly different as to be unreachable. Nothing about him would ever resonate beyond a Hoxton bar with a foreign football theme and fairy lights shaped like chilli peppers. But then there wasn't anything else to look at and all the windows were blacked out by the night.

The conversation extended outwards.

They continued to talk about Geoff, who might be kind, and Alice tried hard to like him for it, to concentrate on his broad shoulders, or to think about the symbolism of a man with large hands, and give him something back. But it was hard. But if she tried hard enough she might just begin to believe it, and Alice Grisham, artist, socialite, and magazine reader, was a believer in belief. She adjusted the belt on her jeans so that the Marc Jacobs label on the belt showed better. She asked Geoff some more questions about Stoke Newington. She got them each another Mojito.

Lara won at table football and Geoff got up to play.

'Are you sure you don't mind?' he said.

'I'm not athletic,' said Alice. It was a line from her favourite Tennessee Williams play. It was a line from. It was a line. There wasn't room for heroes or geniuses anymore, just Che Guevara T-shirts and import Nikes.

I lead a simple life, thought Alice, and stared at the black patent wall of glass.

Geoff went off to play Lara. The other two men sat down with Alice. They bought another round of Mojitos. She had had four now. They talked some more about trainers, particularly about the width of laces, and fatter being better. One of them was a typographer at Dazed. Alice, not being sportswear orientated, stared out at the black as much as politeness would allow. The typographer revealed that he had ordered some new trainers over the internet. He said he had a contact in New York who sent him special trainers you couldn't get here yet. He talked on, until Alice, who could be deliberately amusing when forced, turned away from the window. She responded with an equal depravity of detail and for a brief moment became the life and soul, drunk and grounded and laughing. She liked thin laces she said, for that seventies tennis star look. They laughed and then she laughed and leaned back in her chair. She finished her fifth Mojito.

Lara and Geoff returned from table football and Lara perched herself coyly on the typographers' knee. She wiggled and tossed her hair and the typographer smiled to Geoff and the other man as if he had expected as much and Alice felt concerned for Lara, whom she liked, who had to claim she'd blacked out, who was always a principal, juddering point of focus. They were naïve in different ways.

'I like your jumper,' said the typographer. He was stroking the back of Lara's neck and looking at Alice.

'Thanks. It's cashmere. Pringle,' said Alice, again and with additions.

'Alice loves Pringle,' said Lara for no reason and with little proof and downed the last of a Mojito. She was gleeful and well on her way to being out of it. She let her heel slip out of the ankle boot and then pushed it back in again. 'Are we all ready to go yet?'

They were all ready to go but agreed that they would have to get another round of Mojitos in first. Otherwise they would arrive too early and too sober, and where would be the fun in that? Alice agreed to go too because she was getting into it now, and getting home didn't seem to matter anymore. She was drinking her sixth Mojito and enjoying it. Geoff wanted to play her at table football before they went and Alice finally gave in and said ok.

She scored one goal. Other than that Geoff had completely won.

'I was terrible,' she said and laughed. 'I knew I'd be a bit terrible but that was the next level.' Geoff laughed too.

Alice knew that she had big brown eyes and a slight lisp, and that Geoff probably thought she'd be alright, and probably didn't think beyond it. And it was a shame, for Alice, who believed in extremes. And who might have gone for a drink with the Marquis de Sade. And who wondered what it would be like. And whether or not he'd poison you with Spanish fly. And then start a revolution. And cover you in shit. And then leave you for dead.

And Alice Grisham considered table football, in a trendy Hoxton bar, far, far, outside the realms of taste and decency. Oh! A terrible shame on all of you!

She tried hard to edge her impression of Geoff into either like or dislike but it wouldn't budge either way. It was so useless that she gave in and smiled. They were still stood by the table football table and Geoff, interpreting the gesture differently, moved round behind her.

'You need to do it more like this.' And put his big hands on her smaller ones.

She felt a strange wistfulness for a generic youth club never experienced, and also a growing aversion for gestures inappropriate to their age group - for a type of mock-innocence akin to a grown woman wearing her hair in bunches and pretending not to know. But perhaps, more soberly, this was more her problem than Geoff's. Perhaps she would decide to like him after all, throw a book at his head, and then giggle behind her hand. And then pension plans and starter homes would follow. An engagement ring from Argos payable in instalments and an understandable life of routine patterns, routine aspiration. To think that she had thought their red wine stained, black-toothed mouths revealed a pact with Dionysus, that the overflowing ashtrays constituted a joyful sprint towards the cliffs' edge. Perhaps she could place a pointed toe firmly on his neck, lean in, slit his throat, and watch while the blood spit-gurgled to a slow and cinematic death.

Alice sighed inwardly against a black mirror. Vertigo. They went back over to join the others.

Someone had got another round of Mojitos in, and they carried on warm and redly drinking. They worked out how to get to the party, which was in South London and not on the tube, and someone looked in an A-Z. Someone suggested that they should probably get a cab as they all knew what a nightmare the night buses were. They all agreed.

After a seventh Mojito Lara phoned one on her mobile. The taxi took its time, and Alice also got through another Mojito. Alice thought first that brown sugar did taste different to other sugar, and then that she didn't have any money for the taxi fare. Geoff kept talking to her and she kept smiling obligingly. Lara kept talking and laughing, all of a wriggle, shake and flash. The other men kept watching Lara. More drinks. Redder faces.

Eventually the taxi came and they headed off. Alice reflected that there was always a party and new people to meet whenever you wanted it. And that the new people were often like other people you had met once before. That there was always everything whenever you wanted it, and someone kind and willing to pay. To pull you up and take you higher, up and away and along, just so long as you expected it, and didn't say 'yes' or 'no'. It was one of the best things about London. About being young in London. Clink and chink and ready laughter. The click of a heel. Sweat and perfume and Lara laughing with her head thrown back and a mouth full of fillings. They were all young and going to a party. A great party, full of people like them, but a bit different.

Cinema

She could see him sat on the other side of a misted-up window, a little older than she was, a good haircut and something soft about the mouth. He looked firstly at his watch, and then at nothing in a way that was unperturbed.

Alice stood rigidly still and breathed hard. She was already a badmannered twenty minutes late, but she *had* moved a foot in the direction of the doorway, and then raised a hand to tap the window-pane. She *had* meant to go inside, and it was only the inexplicable panic that followed these small actions, the all too familiar rising sickness, which held her back from actually doing so.

Instead she crossed the road and began to watch him through a shop window opposite. It seemed like the more logical option. Just to gain a little distance and watch him (through two sets of windows) for a bit first. Then, when she felt calmer, they could share an adult drink. Alice wound a loose strand of hair too tightly round her finger, which turned a darker pink, and then let it go again. She began touching the buttons on her blouse in agitated repeat, and wondered how long he'd sit it out.

A pikey-looking teenage couple moved in front of the window and blocked her view. They had been arguing. The girl, who had a very high, scraped back ponytail, sulked and flicked through a stack of tourist postcards, red-eyed. Her boyfriend pulled at her sleeve –

'I don't understand why you're so moody,' he said. 'I love you. I fuck you. I buy you stuff.' He waved a postcard in front of her as proof. 'I don't understand.' Neither did Alice. It seemed a reasonable view to take.

Alice managed to edge round them and continue spying out of the window. At least two minutes had passed and still he was sitting there. The teenage girl glared firmly at a postcard of Tower Bridge. She had awful skin. Alice thought, more calmly, about the detergent-free facewash that was on special offer in Boots. She looked at the girl and the boy and out of the window. A Chinese woman asked several times if they needed any help. Alice feigned interest in a fan.

After five minutes he upped and left, just the same as he ever was. There was release from a tightness in her chest as Rory Brown's perfectly nice, normal back retreated round the corner.

Alice went inside the Curzon Soho, and ordered a gin and tonic. She noticed that each table housed a single twenty-something, most of who had styled themselves as intellectuals, and that often they were pretending to read books. They gave sly glances to other book-reading actors and then pretended to be upset at being caught. Victims to a moment never experienced, caught up in a web of unsubstantiated noir-ish looks and yet unknowing of this – blissfully lacking in insight and safely cocooned in their various pretensions. It seemed stupid to be doing this, thought Alice, sitting alone in a fantasy, when it was already the bar for an actual cinema. Why not go and see an *actual* film and have an *actual* wank instead? Unless of course the style was social isolation. An intellectual style. A boring style. Alice's style was fashion. It was just that sometimes she *was* intellectual. It was a different thing entirely.

She noticed that the staff had new t-shirts. She noticed that her nails were chipped and tapped them against her glass for no reason. She stared back at the glass, and wondered, without conviction, how many gin and tonics it would take to drink oneself to death. She wondered if one ought to forgo the tonic.

My favourite drink is a Martini, thought Alice, *but only in the correct glass.* The thought stayed with her for some time. She wondered if a Martini was kitsch or sophisticated or both. She wondered it dimly, through an under water cloud of faint emotion. A man and a woman together - what did that actually *mean*?

She tapped her fingers against the glass and wondered what films were going to be on at the Curzon next month. Probably something by Godard. Alice liked Godard as Alice liked the cinema. Her favourite of his films was called *Vivre Sa Vie*:

> *Vivre Sa Vie - My Life to Live -* is the story of a beautiful, bored, young woman, played by Anna Karina, who eventually becomes a prostitute. The audience watches as she spends a lot of time drinking alone in bars and coffee shops, socially isolated and charming to strangers. She encounters pimps and philosophers. Wears eyeliner. Dances to records. Her clothes and manners go steadily down hill as the film progresses and she sells herself for less and less. Towards the end however, it looks as though, having unexpectedly found love with a handsome young artist, she will leave her sordid past behind her and build a new life. Unfortunately she is shot twice and dies in the gutter of a suburban street before this can happen. It is the very last scene, sad but also funny.

At the time of the film Godard and Karina were married. Alice thought it seemed strange to cast your wife as a prostitute. She tapped her fingers against her glass and moved her hair out of her eyes and tapped her fingers against her glass.

'Hiya!' A shriek cut through the daze. Alice made out the face of someone she was meant to know. A girl from the year above her at college. Different department. Sculpture maybe. Possibly pleasant. Possibly demented.

'Uh yes?'

'Well... how are you?!'

Her name was Marion or Mary or something and the words flew out with unwarranted delight. As a general rule Alice viewed over-enthusiastic people with suspicion, preferring to limit her own rare fervour to objects, but she was probably pleasant - the dislike being grounded in the triviality of personal taste.

The girl gushed on at speed - new films, old friends, Nicki and Sam in *Time-Out* even, Sam in an exhibition with Jeremy Deller, how she was moving to East London to become more creative and did Alice know of a room that was going? People who were her sort of people? And other stuff too, densely woven in an overwhelming mesh of references - ill-conceived sound-bite statements delivered too quick to be caught up on - and unconsidered clothes. Alice thought hard, they couldn't have had more than a couple of conversations last year, and even then they must have been night-out ones, shouted over the music, not taking it in. She was someone else's friend not hers, or maybe no ones and therefore everyone's. Or maybe she'd slept with Chris.

It would be wonderful to be sectioned, thought Alice. She pictured a high, clean bed. A friendly nurse to spoon-feed her pureed meals and administer a sedative. Just to lie back and give in...

The girl talked on at an immense pace, pushing in her over-achievements and demands to be liked and twice she misused a word.

Alice had learnt, over time, that when this sort of thing happened it was best to maintain continual surprise. Alice tried to penetrate the fog of the girl's gush through an expression of raised eyebrows. She nodded mutely and smiled. It was something about college, then an exhibition, then something about a book –

'I'm reading this!' – and then the book pushed wincingly close to her face. Something familiar but not take-inable. Something styled as intellectual. Alice smiled harder for want of something to say. She felt an irrational fear that this other girl was about to reach out, touch her hand and cause her to scream very, very loudly. Alice smiled hard - thought of institutionalised meals and bed-linen, all of which, she was sure, would be *white* - and the unknown, other girl smiled back.

My favourite drink's
A martini but only
In the correct glass.

(It was a haiku, but not a revelation. Alice already knew she was poetic.)

They talked vaguely and exchanged mobile numbers. She was in an important show that Alice must see. She would put her on the mailing list. Did Alice have an e-mail? A mobile phone? A land line? These days it was so easy to stay in touch! It appeared as though yet another one of her contemporaries was doing fantastically well and keen to let her know about it.

'I feel bitter when I hear about success,' said Alice. It came out thickly, crushed by the crow black murder of other people's accomplishments.

'It must be hard,' said the supposedly successful Marion/Mary, 'there used to be days when I felt so old, but hang on in there!'

It was delivered with cheerleader-like dementia, and the cold, dead smile of a crocodile. Alice glanced at her shoes for reassurance, and her eye latched onto the buckle detail. She wished desperately for a Valium, a sedative, any sedative. Not to be giddy and wide-eyed with euphoria, but to subdue time. To stop it, ignore it, slow it down to a chemically induced snail's pace til it could no longer bother you. Because although Alice liked most drugs, appreciated the fashionable highs and distortions of an occasional Class A, it was actually the subtle, semi-legal ones that attracted her the most. The ones that ever so slightly smoothed or jolted, and enabled you to do the small stuff. Ones like coffee or alcohol or Valium – even Sulphadine Max had a certain charm – ones bought over the counter and implying a sensible, good for the health level of everyday altered perspective. Oh, to be drugged up to the eyeballs on mother's little helpers while Rory Brown gently slipped it in...

And as we observe our heroine now, at this typical, downbeat instant, we see a pink-complexioned girl, with the kind of skin that marks easily and registers embarrassment. A woman corrupted by film, who once had hopes of becoming a great painter, who expects an orchestral accompaniment each time she crosses the road and the heavens to part because she is loved. What would happen if she dared to name and voice her true ambitions? What would she become? She looks fearfully at another woman of the same age and similar background and understands the implications. She taps her toe and hums a little. Stares into the sublime void of polished leather and blanks out the intruder - a poor and unfashionable imitation of reality. *Shit. Life.* It leaves her weak...

'I am working on a fourth painting,' says Alice, and fights back a glazing over, 'but I might become a cinema usherette.'

In one scene at the beginning Anna Karina goes to the cinema. Prior to this she had had hopes of becoming a great actress, but after seeing the already great actresses of the silver screen, in this case Jean Seberg playing Joan of Arc, she changes her mind and becomes a prostitute instead. At the film's opening she has a husband, a son and a job in a trendy record shop, but she leaves them all to pursue a dream of nothingness. Gradually their meaning fades away from her. She walks with a blank stare through seedy streets, listless, and separate from memory. She pouts with her thick-lipped, cock-sucking mouth, drinks spirits, and blags money from men for cigarettes. Staring into the sublime void of Gauloise smoke, she blanks-out all intrusions – *je suis responsible* is her only comment, and sad eyes look away...

The woman talked on. Alice ignored her in order to stare at a half-empty gin and tonic, a film programme and a dirty ashtray. *I am not normal*, she thought, an unwilling and queasy existentialist, and the observation was so mundane it made her want to cry.

Art

The Barbican Centre toilets were less crowded than initially appeared; the walls, in fact, were cleverly mirrored, and the inhabitants therefore numbered five, not twenty-five, well-dressed identikit young women. After a while Alice became conscious that one of them was trying to talk to her. It was Lara's acquaintance, who wasn't a model but wanted to be. There was something recognisable about her, just as there was something recognisable about all of them, and it occurred to Alice that they had probably met at least once before. The Nearly-Model had clearly had the same thought but in order to stave off the embarrassment of neither knowing quite where nor how, merely offered Alice a friendly line. Alice, of course, put down her eyeliner and accepted.

The Nearly-Model checked her nose for powder traces, turned round, and leaned a white denim behind against the wash-basin. She was certainly attractive, but possibly fat with her clothes off. Alice noticed the beginnings of a cold sore halfway across her glossy top lip and that, strangely, this didn't look too bad.

'Which of the indie-boy muscle-boys in the show's yours then?' she asked, peering down at her left tit and then shifting it slightly to the right. 'Which high-achiever are you after?'

She ran a confrontational finger over the top button on Alice's shirt, half-smiling, a proud little puppy routinely playing the femme fatale.

'Geoff,' said Alice, soon to be scatty with the coke, still scatty with the thick spit and flush of every night's pedestrian debauchery, and now noticing a dubious row of cigarette burns peeking out from the girl's waist-band, 'Well I mean I know him. Kind of. I met him the other week. I know him through Lara. Actually, I'm more her friend really.'

'Oh, okay. That's cool.' She removed her hand from Alice's shirt and edged back towards the mirror. 'I guess you must know Nikki and Sam, then. They used to work with this guy I used to see, a photographer, but he's more into fashion than art. Know him? Yeah? Good necklace by the way' – a heavy jet collage of triangles held in place by chrome thread scaffolding – 'just loving your geometry!'

The Nearly-Model began to neaten her mouth with a mixture of Blistex and Juicy Tubes lip-gloss, finished, smiled a sticky goodbye, and then left. Alice resumed correcting her eyeliner, crayoning back and forth and carelessly smudging. She paused to take off the necklace, hold it up against the concrete and mirrors, to twist it this way and then that, creating a, muted, angular kaleidoscope. She did one more circle with the black – she could do it all day but always the same result – and then headed back to the private view. The bar was only free for another half an hour and she was still entitled to a paper cup of luke-warm chardonnay.

The Curve gallery was crowded. Geoff and some other men who looked a bit like Geoff were talking the 'crazy shit' they'd been known to talk, and sorting out the pills for later. Sometimes the other men complimented him on his paintings, repeating things they had read in Frieze magazine, or remembering that his name had been linked with someone listed in the new *Time-Out Art Issue*, while Geoff easily accepted the praise. There were some girls she knew that Lara knew that looked a bit like her and Lara. She joined them.

'Hiya,' said another girl that Alice remembered meeting but couldn't quite place, 'do you know how to get inside this indoor garden then? Apparently there's one somewhere, and we're all just dying to get in and do the neo-hippy thing.' She laughed and put her arm round Alice's waist in a kindly manner and handed her a pill.

'Yes,' said Alice, who was pleasantly surprised. Who had been to the indoor garden on a number of occasions. Who genuinely loved the small scale exoticism of bamboo against city grey, the Koi Carp swimming lazily in their concrete pools, and the fact the garden had *stairs*. She liked the room filled with cacti in particular, where all types of spikes, small and prickly with a lion-cub's danger, jostled for space in an architecturally seminal conservatory/gallery-extension - and the fact you had to go *up stairs* to get there. 'Yes' said Alice, who did, who had been, who had loved, 'you have to come on one of the special Sundays in the summer when they have a concert there, but sometimes they'll let you in on another day if you ring up and are really polite and make an appointment.'

The girl nodded, taken aback by the unexpectedly informed response. *Cacti*, thought Alice, looking at a triangle, a thought-out and contained shape, *cacti*. One felt temporarily rational here, with the thought of nature present yet controlled, the paintings in tiny, accessible doses. She said something suitably pleasant and random about Geoff's picture to her new party friend, extracted herself, and went to the bar.

It took some time to get the drinks. A famous female art critic was getting a ticking-off by the waitress for trying to put two bottles of red in her bag without paying, while her companion, a blond lecturer approaching forty, an ex-indie-boy muscle-boy, was enjoying being out with his students a little too much. Steven Gontarski and Kirsten Glass were trying to talk to the critic about a Kate Bush revival night at the ICA over the top of the ticking-off waitress. Every now and then a stack of beer bottles toppled over and the art students scuttled away from the lecturer and then back again like a sewer full of drunken rats. Alice looked back at Geoff, talking to someone who looked a bit like Gary Webb.

Alice carried the two drinks - wine for herself, a bottle of Becks for Geoff - back over to the boys who looked a bit like each other and the girls who looked a bit like her.

'Great necklace!' said a different loved-up girl to the one from before.

'Cheers,' said Alice, 'it's you know, like, well geometry.'

Everybody laughed. Alice swallowed her pill, swilled down with the cheap white wine.

'I think my paintings are well in on the geometry tip,' said Geoff, basking in his own warm glow of ego and referring to a wonky equilateral in Yves Klein blue, 'I think it's the way forward.'

Everybody laughed again.

'If we can't get into the garden,' said Someone Else who obviously didn't want to get into the garden, 'then there's a good after-party. Some rich kid in a really bling tracksuit organised it,' they pointed out a boy who'd been to Eton dressed head to toe in white and gold Adidas 'everyone gets a goodie bag with a free copy of Art Review and Polly Staple's going to DJ.'

'What's she going to play?' said loved-up girl number one.

'Destroy All Monsters,' said Someone Else, 'it's going to have a very Eighties West Coast feel.'

Everybody nodded.

'But can't we still try and get in the indoor garden?' said Alice, still no closer to being sportswear orientated, still craving something other. 'There might be a way. I mean, what about the neo-hippy thing?'

'You want the garden?' said Geoff, draping one arm around her shoulder in an attempt to pull her back into the present, his inane and successful face pressed against hers. Alice silently nodded. *Yes*, she wanted the garden, traditional pictorial values and the romance of the dark. *Yes*, from the Grisham contingent, a whole-hearted resounding and silent *yes*. 'But babe, that whole indoor garden thing's a bit sci-fi, a bit, you know, the world's ending let's plant stuff. And now there's this really cool after-party! So,' his big face loomed close again, 'let's just be fun people and go to the fun party with the drugs babe-ey.' He made a peace sign, half-ironic and in keeping with the West Coast feel, 'let's just chill out, make like trees and leave!'

Everybody laughed. Geoff shook Alice slightly in his new, funny style, and then began to laugh, and to talk more bollocks to the men who looked like him. As did the girls who looked like Alice. Alice nodded sullenly at Geoff, and temporarily joined in with the girls. They talked mainly about painting, and sometimes a designer sale off Brick Lane. It was only on for a couple of days, but you could get PPQ jeans for a quarter of the price. It was agreed that painting wasn't dead anymore because beauty was making a resurgence and that colour theory was also big news. While the agreements continued the girl who was nearly a model walked up and placed her hand lightly on Alice's waist, then leisurely let it slip down to Alice's arse, keeping it there, looking at Alice then looking at Geoff, who still had his arm round Alice's shoulder. Slowly she licked her cold-sore blemished lips and waited for a response until, not getting one, she eventually moved her hand away.

'I still think we need to sort out the drugs before we leave,' said the bloke who had first mentioned the after-party. 'Will there be any there?'

The boy in the really bling tracksuit who had been to Eton had come over to join them. He patted Geoff on the back and murmured something about the reinvented blue before putting his arm around the Nearly-Model.

'Yeah we've got loads of MDMA powder,' he offered too eagerly.

The Nearly-Model smiled. Geoff smiled. Alice forced her mind to wander. She thought about some of the things she liked. These included dark chocolate with cherries, a second-hand china cat, Jean-Paul Belmondo and the smell of French vanilla.

'What's MDMA powder?' said Alice, reluctant to mention her real interests, concerned that they would be as unappreciated as the garden.

'It's like the best bit of an E, but without any of the smackieness, no ketamine or anything, just really pure,' said Geoff. Big smile at Alice. Big smiles all round.

'And some Charlie obviously,' said the kid in the tracksuit. More smiles.

'I want to get so wrecked,' said Geoff, squeezing Alice harder, smiling like a madman, 'I just want to get, like, really wrecked.'

Alice sighed and tried to physically shrug Geoff off. *Perhaps the Nearly-Model can help him out later*, thought Alice, releasing herself from the obligation of Geoff through a genuine search for alternatives, *perhaps she has more to give and perhaps she loves to give it*. She sighed again.

'Hey babe-ey,' said Geoff, who had still never been American, 'what's with all the intensity?' He put his shrugged-off arm back in place, firmly, territorially, out of habit and not really giving a fuck. 'You look kind of Chekhov-like, shit this is terrible get me back to Moscow. Do any of you guys know Alice's friend Camilla? She's having a party with a Russian theme. Save that face for then babe, save the misery for Russia.'

'A Russian theme?' said Someone Else. 'What do Russians wear?'

'I think it's quite a poor country,' said the Nearly-Model for no real reason, smiling back at Geoff.

'Why's it poor?' said Someone Else, with the same lack of reason as the Nearly-Model.

Perhaps she has something *to give.*

'They're not all poor,' said loved-up girl number one, 'some of them are loaded. They have some really cool bars there, full of entrepreneurs in Dolce & Gabana. I read about it in *i-D.*'

Everybody nodded. The rich kid in the tracksuit suggested that his tracksuit would go down well in Russia. Everybody nodded again. Geoff began to gently rub Alice's arm and to talk confidently to everybody again about his use of blue. Everything was a mirror of everything else with a dirty loved-up voice whispering success. Everything was a toilet mirror, reflecting non-stop in a distant arctic glare.

'I'm sorry,' said Alice, 'but I feel suddenly very sick.'

Realistically, there was hardly any time left before the E kicked in. That meant hardly any time left to find a cash-point, a taxi, and mutter directions home to a potential rapist with little or no grasp of the English language.

'I'm sorry,' said Alice, the conscious victim of a superfluous education and aesthetic sensibility. 'I've had a lovely time, but I really must be going.'

She began, while putting on her coat, to think again, very carefully and deliberately, about some of the things she liked. By the smell of French vanilla, she had reached the top button, and with it said a temporary goodbye to a learned helplessness.

Kenwood House

Then a March. The season changed and, briefly, so did Alice. She chose to embrace the melodrama of despondency with renewed vigour; bought tubes of acrylic bright with intent, filled out many, reckless applications, and then, one day, set off in search of an unseen Vermeer. Rumour had reached her of its existence – a north London stately home set in landscaped surrounds, filled heavy with oil paint and frequented by pensioners.

And surely each of us has fallen prey to unfashionable, inanimate compulsions in our time, be it childhood toy or steel-heeled shoe? Felt the shaman's lifeless magnetic pull at Topshop Oxford Circus? Viewed the dark delights of a specialist publication or felt a heavy piece of silk and thought how superior to skin? And this being so, these desires acknowledged and accepted in our modern world, then why shouldn't Alice be drawn to historic buildings? Polished floors? Why not fetishise gilt-edges, canvas squares – the real reproduced, composed, distilled, in loving layers of ochre wash?

Alice chose not to approach the house by what she took to be the standard route, but unwittingly her path was one of only a contrived neglect. The landscape dated from a time when the gentry wished to experience the charm of a rural idyll from the comfort of their own estates, and they designed their gardens accordingly. She remembered, smiling, the tale of a wealthy aesthete who had commissioned the building of a miniature abbey on his grounds, and then hired a man to live there dressed as a hermit. She thought of Marie-Antoinette provoking outrage with her high fashion milk-maid's attire, and at the same time noted that the architecture was Neoclassical. Her journey took a while, with this build-up of dramatic musings, nature and the wind; until, finally, arrival, and with it a jolt of door-framed stillness.

Alice pictured how she must look to other people – an English Rose in a dark wood frame, an observed form centrally placed at a designated distance in a roped off area - and couldn't remember when she had last been so pleased. It was frightening, and she felt safer once inside as the happiness concentration lessened. She removed her coat (Sonia Rykiel), adjusted her jumper (John Smedley), and then found a painting that looked the same as copies she had seen in books:

> On the right, quite casually, one arm in fact cut short by the frame, as though maybe Vermeer wasn't *quite* concentrating when it came to the composition, sits a girl dressed in buttercup yellow:
>
> A velvet jacket trimmed with ermine
> A full, rustling, skirt, in the same, though slightly duller, colour
> A string of pearls, discreet enough for a woman who might be wealthy but is also young
>
> And a lightly painted, almost impressionistic face-
>
> With teeth that bite the bottom lip
> And pale hands to tentatively hold a mandolin

Her eyes flit to the space past the curt and cut-off line and stay there.

Waiting for a teacher's guidance
One hidden beyond the clumsy edges?
Or just waiting - the image *should* be about the waiting –

The waiting and the watching and the innocent, slanting look.

But it's landscape that demands centre stage.
Framed trees which usurp the sitter's place
Alongside the murky books, towards the left, already loosing definition.

And then it fades out altogether.
Into dark shadow...

With so much left unfinished.

Alice smoothed her hair and stared intently. She took in the yellow, which she thought uplifting, the mood, which she thought decorous, and practiced a particularly emotive sigh – which through rehearsal became the act itself. She sighed, gloriously alone, consumed by the elation of possibility.

'I didn't know you liked Vermeer but I suppose it, err, makes sense,' said Rory Brown, halting the trance. He made a vague circular movement in front of the painting as if to acknowledge both the yellow and the fur.

'The Guitar Player' said Alice, although he most likely knew already, and if he didn't there was a card beneath to tell him. She was off guard and blushed slightly. 'I didn't expect to see you.'

'Likewise,' said Rory with a smile approaching wry. Infinite politeness prevented any mention of the Curzon's non-liaison however. Instead, they discussed colour theory – Rory said he associated yellow with jaundice – and walked round Kenwood House.

They paused in front of a Reynolds. Alice remembered that Rory was sweet, and the moment became one for confidences.

'I'm thinking of becoming a cinema usherette,' she said.

'Really?' Rory smiled, understanding, indulgent, 'will you have your own torch?'

'I might do, and I'll have a uniform and sell ice creams on a tray round my neck. Definitely a uniform. A good one.'

'What type of uniform?' He was always encouraging, guileless, and not the type to take the piss.

'I don't know yet. Something with stripes, and a bow maybe?'

'Yeah I can see that. Very Hopper. And what type of films will be on?'

'Old ones.'

They looked at Turner and Gainsborough. Rory had a soft spot for figurative painting because Rory was educated and Rory was soft. They looked at the library. They looked at the Orangerie, no longer the spot where painted ladies used to stroll on rainy days, but a gift shop, the walls, courtesy of National Heritage, now coloured to match the costumes in the portraits – lilac to compliment Lady Suchabody's dress, red and grey for Rembrandt's head-wrap and robe. Rory asked after some of Alice's friends who were also his friends, in particular their friend Armond, who had recently been to hospital, and their friend Camilla, who had been his friend first.

'I'm thinking of doing an MA at the Courtauld,' said Rory, who like many of her friends who were also his friends had also once planned to be a painter, 'but maybe it's too old-fashioned. There's also a curation course at Goldsmiths that I'm considering. That's more theory based'

'I'd go to the Courtauld,' said Alice. 'There's too much theory about as it is. Besides, it's very now to be vintage, and beauty is having a resurgence.'

She was only half regarding him and toyed with her hair as she spoke.

From one window there was what looked like a pretty bridge across a pond. She wanted them to walk towards it. She suggested that they do so now.

'It's not a real bridge, it's a folly,' said Rory, but sensing her disappointment quickly added, 'perhaps we could walk over to the folly?'

They obliged each other and walked over to the bridge that was a folly. *Why build a fake bridge?* thought Alice. She was quietly amused by such a small and unnecessary counterfeit, a 2D cut-out painted in trompe l'oeil – hardly the grandest of dreams – and let her heels sink into the soft mud. She prised off a piece of bark with once clean fingernails, and felt awake in the still wetness of March outdoors. The wood was black-brown. She and Rory smiled at each other, and Alice threw her head back and laughed, and it was just for happiness not even for a proper reason. She took a skipping step, slipped, and softly, in slow motion, inelegantly fell. The damp earth ground into the wholesome Britishness of pleated wool, twigs snagged her stockings, and what else could she do but kick up her legs in feigned distress, and then laugh again, harder, overcome. She reached out both her arms, and Rory pulled her up. He laughed. They both laughed. They both smiled.

The back of an expensive skirt was smeared burnt umber. Alice had got some mud on her hands. She held them out in front of her and examined the gritty nailed damage.

'You're all muddy,' said Rory. He had soft eyes.

'I am yes.' They were both full up on too much weird laughter. 'There's a tearoom round the back.'

Inside the tearoom Alice took off her coat and wiped her hand on the back of her skirt, which was already past saving. Rory placed his well-cut, good quality jacket on the back of his chair. It was an understated jacket, made from navy needle-cord so as to reference the modern academic.

'Let's share a cake,' said Rory, the giver.

'Oh, yes please,' said Alice.

Rory went away and came back with an airy mound of sponge and jam. There were cheap cherries and a fat blob of butter cream. Alice quickly devoured her half, getting jam, too, on the wool skirt. Jam and mud – it was a strangely comforting combination. Then she licked her jammy, earthy fingers. She drank some of her tea and leaned back in her chair. She was full and comfortable.

'So do you think you'll buy a yellow dress?' said Rory. When he smiled it was pleasant. He had shiny brown hair that was cut to look casual.

'Might do. Might look jaundiced.' They both laughed. 'Did you like the Vermeer?'

'Not that one so much, but others. The simplicity. He's an intelligent painter without pretension. I don't think you can ask for more than that. You like it?'

'That one, but not so much the others. I think I usually like what you'd expect me to like.'

'Would you like to share a second cake?' said Rory, and Alice laughed. The sun shone in brightly through the window. A sparrow flew into the glass, but then fluttered off again unhurt. Alice searched in her bag for change because Rory shouldn't have to pay for both the cakes. A hand scraped amongst coins and fluff, and then inadvertently she exposed herself.

A tube of cobalt blue had fallen out. It lay guiltily amidst the crumbs.

'The fourth painting?' said Rory who already knew too much, but never judged.

'Yes but we mustn't talk about it. There's been too much talk.' Alice fumbled with her bag, but let the paint lie there. It looked nice gainst the tabletop. The white enamel tube with its little blue square. The plate with the crumbs. It looked painterly.

Rory went to buy the second cake. His jacket fell onto the floor when he stood up, and Alice picked it up and put it back on his chair for him. She brushed some dust from the tailored sleeve in a way that was affectionate. Rory came back with the cake, and Alice lifted it off the plate and took a bite before he had had time to put the tray down.

'Bored women turn to the fridge. I'm going to get fat,' she said. Her voice was deep with the stodge.

'No you're not,' said Rory, 'you look like you've lost weight. You look nice.'

They began to finish off the second cake between them. Another bird banged up against the glass, maybe it was the same bird, and then flew away again. Rory was a tidy eater and ate less than Alice. He didn't make any crumbs or spill things. Alice began to play with her hair; she piled it up on top of her head, then let it fall back down to her shoulders again. She did this several times. A small sigh.

'What about Fragonard?' she said after a while. 'He's sometimes pretentious and not always clever. Do you like him?'

'Well I can see why *you* like Fragonard,' said Rory. He chewed a slow mouthful of cake and looked thoughtful, 'but people can still relate to Vermeer. The homeliness. People look at Vermeer and sense tranquillity.' He took another spongy mouthful, 'you seem happy at the moment.'

'I think it's the sunshine.' She turned her head towards the window and saw that it had turned a cloudy grey. They both laughed. 'Is that what people want then, tranquillity?'

'It's what a lot of people want. It doesn't make them stupid.'

'No it doesn't,' said Alice. They smiled at each other. They understood. All the cake was gone and they sat in silence for a time. After a while Rory shifted nervously in his seat.

'What are you doing now?' he said. 'If you wanted you could come back to mine. Watch a film or something.'

The emphasis lay on the something.

'I don't know,' said Alice. She scrabbled clumsily with the paint tube and shoved it back in her bag, 'lots to do.'

'Oh. Okay. Maybe see you around, then?'

'Oh. Yeah. Yeah. Okay. That'd be nice.'

'Nice?' He looked upset, almost sarcastic, 'yeah, okay. It'd be *nice*.'

They said goodbye. Rory left first, and then Alice put her coat on and went outside. It was sunny again. As soon as she was sure that he was safely out of sight, she started running. She ran most of the way back across the heath towards the train station. She fell once, sat there in the mud for a moment, and then ran off again. She wasn't used to running; she was used to standing still, and the cold wrench for breath stung the back of her throat. She would keep running, through the mud and the clouds. She was a painter in the landscape. This meant something. The sky was the colour of the paint.

Technique

Alice applied for a travel scholarship. Then forgot about it. Time passed in the manner to which she had become accustomed until one day, much to her astonishment, she was invited for an interview.

A genuine chance for advancement moved within her field of vision and brushed against her with gentle fingertips, hinting at fulfilment. She would be expected to present her work and self in a coherent manner in just three weeks hence, and to convince an unknown congregation of her intelligent candour. In times of need, when sensing a lack, one sought salvation and turned to a decent man.

'So you want me to Photoshop these slides?' said John.

They were stood in his Hoxton office. Sometimes Alice popped by on her way to and from the Liverpool Street Starbucks and had another coffee. John worked part-time at an art magazine for not much money and a good C.V. He was surrounded by Apple Macs with flat screens and printed-out press releases. He had access to this equipment and understood it, put the theory into practice and clicked and flicked purposefully *towards* something. Alice was a Luddite by comparison, attempting to smash technology through indifference, or a medievalist even, preferring illusions and tricks of the light. Technical skills, in Alice's opinion, wheedled their way in and gave a freedom not always deserved, cutting, cropping and in due course flattening, removing the drips and thumb prints that leant claim to authorship and therefore immortality. Saint Alice the Romantic, owner of a drawer filled with dark and dust flecked slides. She put her fingers in her ears and floated off the edge of the world, frightened and digitally inept. She expected that her death would be caught on a camera phone, and then viewed over the internet two clicks away from a quadruple penetration.

John, on the other hand, didn't have any fears. On the other hand, John *did* have five fingers, with which manly digits he moved his iPod off the desk. He rearranged booklets and papers in the precarious manner of the warehouse washing-up. He brushed the seat of an office swivel chair, motioned for Alice to take a seat, and typed something into the computer.

'What's that?' asked Alice. A photograph of John's art work and a short biography had flashed up across the screen.

'It's called Bowie Art,' said John proudly.

'Bowie Art? As in David Bowie?'

'Yeah. It's an "online" gallery,' he made a movement with his fingers to symbolise the use of punctuation, then blushed at the geeky gesture. 'You get put in exhibitions and stuff. And meet the other Bowie artists.'

'How'd you get David Bowie to look at your work?' asked Alice. She was impressed. She'd been to art-school, and like every outsider she knew about Bowie. He was savage and changeable, terrifyingly cool, and close to a God – an image in a magazine seen often and long enough to become part of her own everyday. Why wasn't she on Bowie Art?

'Well, David Bowie doesn't look at *everything* himself. He has a team. Actually, it costs eighty quid so you can be on it if you like,' said John, who clicked and flicked with decent purpose. 'It'd be a good career move,' he added, clicking off Bowie Art and back to Photoshop.

Oh! The shame! The shame! Oh! The terrible desperate shame! John drove his car to the big Tesco and bought organic herbs from Spain. John focused on one thing at a time and slowly but surely, tank-like, gained ground – a little shudder from the unenlightened.

'Cold?' said Saint John the Decent, and delivered a friendly slap to the shoulder. Alice shook her head and gave him a look that alluded to perky. John was a genuinely good person.

And, after six months of lethargy, Alice had an interview for a travel scholarship – eligibility for a year's holiday in Rome. There wasn't one for Russia and, as Alice had decided her approach was more European, this was in fact better. The award paid for twelve months accommodation and living expenses – a term which seemed foolishly unclear to someone who had recently seen *La Dolce Vita* at the NFT. Inactivity had turned Rome into a paradise, and London in the present therefore became a purgatory. The interview panel, an official intelligentsia who would call judgement on Alice's unpoliced desires, a no lesser power than the God of Calvin. And because everything now rested on this one event, because everything in Alice's life, she now realised, had been a prelude to this occurrence, disaster loomed close at hand. Alice bit her lip too hard and drew a little blood. She searched for her remaining slides with the tang of salt and metal, of human transience, in the back of her mouth. John moved the last of the papers.

'What's that?' said Alice. She had noticed a numbered list in John's neat and tidy hand. Number three was Jeremy Deller. Number six was Bowie circa 1975. Other clever, trendy artists made up the rest.

'It's my top ten,' said John. He was nearly embarrassed, 'I was bored.'

'For Artforum?'

'Yeah.'

A different successful, international art star listed their top ten in each edition of Artforum. They explained their choices in one or two informed, sound-bite statements. Sometimes a photograph and a brief biography. Usually it filled one page.

'Thinking ahead,' said Alice, and laughed. John, caught out, laughed too.

Alice was touched, but knew better than to comment. 'Do you think Chris' got his top ten ready?' she said instead.

'Probably,' said John and laughed, properly this time, 'a controversial and aggressive list of heroes and a photo of him scowling.'

Alice laughed too. It was undeniably likely.

'And have you noticed his cross?' said John.

'No? What cross? Where?' said Alice.

'He's started wearing a gold crucifix on a chain. He wants to be a lapsed Catholic of Italian origin. It's this season's look.'

'Guilt complex and everything?' said Alice, 'Persecuted and hounded, and him against the man? Well at least it'll match the hair.'

When viewed from a distance they often found Chris ludicrous, because from a distance they gained a clearer view. John's shoulders shook with silent mirth as he adjusted the iPod's volume.

Alice believed, fierce and necessarily narrow, that things would be different in a foreign city, and that she would be different also. That people would confuse personal difference for cultural, and any eccentricity would hopefully project an English allure. *When I go to Rome I will wear Laura Ashley dresses,* thought Alice, *and when I come back I will wear black and gold and sun glasses.*

'Do you want me to put them on a disk?' said John. He had finished fiddling and was ready to get down to business, 'and how many do you want doing?' he added, getting a decent kick out of knowing more.

'Nine,' said Alice 'they said to bring between ten and twenty, so I've got nine.'

She produced nine terrible slides of three competent paintings from within a crumpled envelope. A leaf also fell out. Alice didn't know where the leaf had come from. John looked appalled but kept quiet. He would enjoy showing Alice how well he could navigate Photoshop.

John ran his hand across his newly shorn scalp and began moving the mouse. He had a low-maintenance, fashionable skinhead haircut that he did himself. He used a special electric shaver and two mirrors, positioned so that he could see the front and the back of his head at once. There was an aura of timeless, reliable masculinity about him. A man's man, like Steve McQueen, who owned an iPod, and could use Photoshop, and could be relied upon.

'Look at this,' he said, passing her a flyer from on top of some papers, 'I can get us free tickets if you want to go.'

It was an Eighties-esque line drawing of a couple dancing in tight jeans, promoting a night at the ICA. Apparently Sadie Coles was going to play compilation tapes with Jarvis Cocker in between sets from Martin Creed's band. The night was entitled *Fuck Dance Lets Art*. It looked very deliberately cool with a scholarly slant.

'Maybe,' said Alice. She turned the flyer over to read about the accompanying digital projections. 'It looks like it's meant to be fun.'

Many of Alice's slides had been taken at odd angles or were slightly out of focus. Some were scratched far beyond recognition, but technology could correct this and passive idealism failed to ruin her. The slides were placed on top of a butch-looking architecture magazine, while John used a tiny brush to get rid of the dirt. Having just escaped a martyr's death, Alice didn't know if she was pleased. She tapped her toe; it was becoming a habit akin to a twitch, looked at the flyer some more, and hummed.

John finished cleaning the slides and scanned them in with the easy charm for which he was well known. He opened a beer. There was always beer at John's office.

'So what do you think you'll get up to in Rome?' he said after a while.

'Get a tan. Have an affair. Go to parties and jump in a fountain!' That was what she had anticipated. In that order. 'Oh and I want to see the view from the Rivoli Bridge.'

'Isn't that in Venice?'

'Oh.'

Italy was a country born from blood and gold. The best for food, for clothes, for architecture. The exact location of the Rivoli Bridge was inconsequential. Alice hoped for discovery. She was politely grateful to John as the conduit. She absolved him for not understanding. When he was older he might be a bit like Cary Grant. She liked Carry Grant best in *North by Northwest*. Liked the way he still looked suave when attacked by a low flying aircraft. Cary Grant, winning a war, unruffled in a well-cut suit...

John had put down a Tesco Metro bag. Inside was a joint of meat and a packet of frozen pastry.

'What's all that for?' said Alice.

'I thought I'd make a Beef Wellington.'

He clicked and dragged the mouse. As a lieutenant in Nam he would have found a way to feed the entire platoon after a long days fighting, and then offered some to those poor gook bastards out the goodness of his heart. Steve McQueen in Nikes winning a war. Alice ate out or else mainly from a tin.

'I always thought I shouldn't cook because I'm an artist.'

'No' said John, 'you cook *because* you're an artist.' He clicked authoritatively on the left mouse button and a black spot disappeared.

'Perhaps I could help with the Wellington?' asked Alice, pleased that John looked pleased. Later they would push and pile the plates together inside their abattoir of taste, and a new level of flour would be sprinkled on top of the old level of grime. Some beef would be eaten. Some left rotting on the side. Click drag. Two slides became transfigured.

'Do you think Rome will change me?' said Alice.

'Well, you'll learn Italian. And the art scene will be less contemporary.' Click drag. John concentrated on the screen and remained unmoved. Rome did not represent anything for him.

'I'm not sure how long to cook the Wellington for,' he said.

'Just 'til it's done,' said Alice. She wasn't listening – a crack in the desk had caught her eye, and remained in her field of vision. She ran her finger over it without thinking. Lately her mind was prone to long spells of blankness. It could latch onto a small thing, an unravelling hem for instance, and then circle it absently for a prolonged stretch of time.

'Emotionally. I meant, will it change me emotionally?'

'I don't know. Do you mean give you different emotions?'

'No. More intense ones. The light will be brighter.'

John chose not to respond. He was clicking and dragging in a concentrated way.

'This is called the feather tool,' he said.

The light in the office was blue white. Some lights were yellow white. It depended on the type of bulb. Alice went on the internet on a neighbouring computer and looked up recipes for Beef Wellington. She thought about the taste of a chocolate she had just eaten.

'It depends on the size,' she said

'What?'

'How long you cook the Wellington for. It depends on the size.'

Alice checked her e-mails. She only had one. It was from Camilla. Camilla had forwarded her a picture of a cat dressed as a cow. It was funny. Alice looked at the Vogue web site with particular reference to hats and took a mouthful out of John's beer. John Photoshopped. She replied to Camilla's e-mail, and then she forwarded the cat/cow picture to Lara along with a weblink to *Fuck Dance Lets Art* at the ICA. Then she looked at a web site on Fellini. Alice clicked through the pages until she found the famous image of the blonde starlet from *La Dolce Vita* frolicking in the fountain. Apparently she had had wellies on underneath her cocktail dress for the whole of the filming. It didn't matter. Alice wondered what the starlet would look like with brown hair and smaller breasts. Then she wondered what she would look like with blonde hair and larger breasts. Then she went back to hats. She clicked between the hats and Italy until they merged into one, and wondered what the Dolce Vita blonde would like in a hat, or with four cocks up her, or what she would look like with four cocks up her or in a hat. Preferably one with a veil.

Fragonard

Jean-Honore Fragonard, indisputable king of the kinky biscuit tin, produced *The Bolt* – twenty-six by thirty-two point five centimetres, oil on canvas – in around 1776. He studied both in Paris under Boucher, to whom he is often – perhaps stupidly – compared, and then in Rome.

Fragonard was an observer of life; the culture of late romantic (the French called it decadent) society held a continual fascination for him. After he had taken in the glory of the Sistine Chapel and the horrors of the Cappuccino Church, and been dwarfed by the bloodied history of the Coliseum and gazed upwards in the Parthenon, Fragonard had seen quite enough of those sort of sights. He returned to his native land in 1761, complete with his very own brand of naughty flattery with which to become the ladies' pet at Court. A position that did not bode well when the revolution came. Fragonard's soft hands and well-to-do connections soon had him up against the wall. He fled to the provinces and, when finally able to return, found the memory of his favourite city a republican ruin. *Poor Fragonard* – the moment on which he'd staked his claim had well and truly passed. He died in penniless obscurity sometime in 1806, while his patrons who'd escaped the guillotine publicly abandoned their frivolous ways, (the fashion was now for one red ribbon tied round the neck momento-mori style). Partying was completely out of vogue.

> *The Bolt* is a small, predominantly yellow, resplendently pre-Revolution painting over half of which is taken up by the rumpled sheets and drapery of a large bed. Over this hangs an outsized orange curtain, swept back to reveal a disarray of sheets and pillows. Beneath it is an opened case, out of which spill various clothes, while in the furthest left hand corner is a yellow covered table with a perfume bottle and what looks like more clothing, although one cannot say for definite because the brushwork is so loose - a haze of pleats and folds.

(Alice has heard of a book called *The Fold: Leibniz and the Baroque*, by a contemporary philosopher called Dealuze. It was on all her reading lists at college, and she thinks that although this probably means it vaguely links to everything, it might also, in some more special way, be linked to *The Bolt*. She considers the cascading fabric especially, heavy with alternations in context and tone. According to Lebinitz it would be made up of monads, meaning one, single, unique thing, meaning the smallest, most basic unit of perceptual reality, and meaning, therefore, that *every* thing – the curtains, the paint, her hand – must consist of this one essence. She hasn't thought beyond this though, and for the time being is merely pleased with the reference to endlessly falling material. Content to mull it over in a public space, one hand cupping her coffee in Godard style obliqueness, the other playing idly with a faux-diamond ring... Alice thinks about Dealuze, who takes-on Leibniz's metaphysical view and runs with it, says that the unconscious is a myth, that 'identity' is in a permanent state of flux – and wonders if she should get into him. He is foreign after all, and apparently committed suicide by jumping from the window of his Paris apartment... She has heard also, via John, that Deleuze's 'end' prompted an essay by a man called Colmbat, entitled *Death as an Event*, where he sets out to define both its historical significance and its place as an incorporeal event in thought. Colmbat writes of it as double-sided, where each side is a constantly moving fissure, separating states of affairs and propositions. *Alive and kicking as a piece of cloth* thinks Alice or, as Deleuze himself might have said, we should not say Deleuze is dead, but Deleuze and Death. Deleuze and Suicide. Or, Alice and a Piece of Cloth. Alice and a Coffee Cup and a Book Called Philosophy. Alice an Event at Three O'clock.)

> A yellow light seems to radiate from the right hand side. There is a footstool, for balance and formality, and also, more importantly, a struggling couple. The man, who is dressed in white shirt and britches, is turned away from us, reaching up on tiptoe, and ramming a bolt into the door. In his arms, facing us, is a woman. She appears to be both trying to stop and to encourage the man, who holds her firmly in place. One hand is reaching in towards his neck as if to fight him, her expression is one of fear, and yet her body presses in against him almost passionately. (What exactly is it that she wants? Victory? Defeat? Or just the fight itself?) In contrast little can be seen of his face other than a swirl of golden curls. He is simply a muscular, daffodil force. Whereas the woman, who is in full view, has a look of the china doll variety no doubt popular at the time, and her lighter gold hair, the same shade as her disordered dress, almost blends into the wall.
> The painting blurs and glows. The yellow sweeps over the whole image. The struggling couple, the door, the bed, all tumble into one flame of light in an ambiguous tussle of desires. A tenderness and brutality best reproduced on a chocolate box - it betrays a tendency towards airport fiction, exposes provincial dreams ...

Around 1777 Fragonard produced another, larger, version for a private collector that now hangs in the Louvre:

> Here the brushwork is clearer and tighter. The perfume bottle has been replaced with an apple and a posy has been dropped on the floor. The walls and table are more white and cream. Almost green sometimes. The drapery a definite red, and the couple no longer blur into one as the man's hair is now dark and therefore disconnected.
> More has been written about this work than the other. We can read that the apple references the temptation of Eve, or how Fragonard's change in style symbolises a move away from Rococo towards the Neoclassical.

Alice has seen this version and is less keen, but mainly due to the changes in colour. Alice, who longs to press her pink cheek against a golden sun, prefers the obscure glow of version one, to the clearly defined version two. Is more drawn towards the indistinct.

Alice likes to stand on one foot and then change onto the other foot. She pushes her hair out of her eyes and behind her ears, and looks at a painting which the past has termed kitsch. She smiles. The fighting is so hopelessly staged. And the yellow is so yellow. It is one of her favourite paintings in London. It is her outright favourite Fragonard. Alice the painter visits it on a regular basis. In part because of the above and a penchant for lacy smut now viewed as outdated and tame, in part because she has been unable to buy it as a postcard.

The Bolt is a recent acquisition to the National Gallery's permanent collection, placed in one of the smaller, more sombre galleries and hung at around head height. Admission is free, the coffee shop adequate.

Part 2

Margate

More time passed. And so now it was April, and now it was spring, and the Hackney Wick collective were all still hopeful. They were young; they were beautiful; they just got in the car and drove. Faster and faster now, into the middle distance, the sunset, and the whole of the glittering night. *It's a crash course for the ravers / It's a drive in Saturday...* Faster and faster now until speed blurs and fades and swirls towards the vortex. Under John's duress they got in the Fiesta and headed for Margate - all of a tumble of angry enthusiasm. It was outside of London, but not too far - an adventure that did not require forward planning - a hedonistic balm for under achievers. And if they didn't do something soon, they might never do anything at all. And it was a trip, and it was the sea, and they would get wrecked and argue and be united.

The car was an extension of the warehouse - unfeasibly dirty and clinging to life. The front bumper was dented, an indicator was partially, inexplicably melted and a blanket smelling of a pet they had never owned. As expected John drove, Chris (who was not on the website) played Bowie (who he was, therefore, still free to like) at an annoying volume, and Alice sat in the back with a magazine.

Ten minutes into the journey they stopped at a service station. Chris bought a scotch-egg bar and John filled up the tank with petrol. The scotch-egg bar was egg reformed into the shape of a bar, stuffed with flavoured gristle and then coated in neon breadcrumbs. It cost seventy pence for two. It was the future. Chris put one whole bar in his mouth at once. He got back in the car before the others could complain and turned the volume up very loud. There was a brief squabble through the window about money and John was forced to assert his authority as a decent man. Guilty children handed over a section of debt and order was temporarily restored. John got back in the car, turned the volume down a notch, placed a key in the ignition, and drove on. Soon they were out on the motorway. John changed into fifth gear like a man who knew his own mind.

Alice removed a loose thread from a new, light grey Pringle jumper and looked out the window. She was also wearing a navy, pleated skirt, knee-high navy and grey argyle socks, pointed white girl's brogues, and a vintage blazer in charcoal grey felt with particularly hard-core pockets. Her hair was in a ponytail tied with a red ribbon, and her scarf and gloves were a matching striped red and navy set. They had been bought especially for the occasion. *Preppy, fun loving, outdoor girl.* There had been something similar in Japanese Vogue. She complimented John who also exuded a fair degree of complementary preppy fun-loving outdoorsness, though in his case it was less deliberate. He was wearing a parka. John looked over his shoulder at Alice and smiled. No one had ever doubted that he would be successful in life.

Chris, who couldn't drive, who hadn't been complemented, whose success was hit and miss, started on the second packet of scotch-egg bars. He had bought two, and the radioactive crumbs fell on his feet. He was wearing a large gold crucifix on a chain, and the back of his neck was re-tinged blue/black from a Mafioso update. Lately he had started saying 'muthafucka,' and then allowed for his bottom lip to tremble almost slyly.

That was the three of them, then. This then, was still the gang.

Alice read out everybody's horoscopes. It was a comfortably familiar day that promised love and destiny. She opened three cans of Stella and passed one to each of the boys. She recalled a Truffaut film where the heroine, who alternated between being the lover of two different men (best friends in fact), finally tired of the well-known angst and drove her car into a lake. It was black and white and set, in places, in the countryside. Chris turned the music up full blast again and wound down the window; he then leaned out and howled loudly like a wolf. John laughed hysterically. He zigzagged the car down the road and briefly took both hands off the steering wheel to light a cigarette. Chris laughed and howled again. Alice laughed and wound her window down as well, squealing with delight. Bowie blared out behind them - *It's a crash course for the ravers / It's a drive in Saturday* - they had only brought the one tape. They all drank beer. Chris threw his scotch-egg bar wrapper out the window. Alice kicked the back of his chair to join in. They were young. They were sweet and still hoped hard for the future:

'Your hair is atrocious', said Alice. 'It's nearly neo-Gothic, but it's too thick.'

'I think the problem's because you don't condition it properly,' said John, who sometimes used a Clinique for Men cleansing facial scrub. 'It's important to use the right products for your type of skin and hair. You should get a conditioner for it if you colour-treat it.'

'Has it got something in it?' asked Alice. She had noticed an extra sheen.

'I have begun using a styling product, yes.'

'A styling product?' John's laughter was almost harsh. 'A product for styling? Which product would that be?'

It was too hilarious. A styling product.

'Wella,' said Alice, 'he uses Shock Waves by Wella because he saw an advert at the cinema. It said, this is what all those hard, spic gangsters use, and you can buy it cheap in Boots.'

Shock Waves by Wella. It was the gypest one she could think of. It was rank.

'Do you use the mousse? Or maybe a strong-hold gel?'

Chris looked hurt. Alice and John laughed harder. They were helpless now.

'And it's always sort of matted. It's kind of like an animal.'

'Quit busting my balls, muthafucka,' he jabbed hard into John's arm causing the car to swerve inadvertently. Something dark hinted at sincerity. He had the edge over them because he understood humour differently. He didn't fear the ridiculous, and would therefore always go that extra step. Chris smiled to himself and looked out the window. He could be very smug.

'Yeah. Don't fuck with him fuck-face,' said Alice.

She was mildly hysterical, as they all were. The shock of leaving the warehouse *en masse* might just push them over the edge. Suddenly they existed in the outside world, in a world outside of London. Locals might abuse them because of their superior clothes. It had happened before. They would have to get in first and raise hell. Go that one step further, just in case. Shattered glass. Chris in A&E. A picture took shape...

But soon they would see the sea and life presented other possibilities. It could be a gentle grey day with ice creams and sand dunes. Out of season and belonging to them.

They made their way towards the beach and, for a few moments, all three were silent before an endless, purposeless expanse of water merged with sky. Whichever way you looked it seemed, however far you walked, the sea stared back, impassive, grey and unrelenting. Lapping forwards and backwards and forwards again. You were small here, always, and to the point of insignificance. You were small.

Then seagull screams cut through the reverie, and they were able to notice, a few meters away, a small kiosk selling mint-choc-chip Cornettos. A father and son chased a plastic football caught by the wind. The father earnest and out of breath, the boy tumbling and circling, arms out from his sides to mimic an aeroplane.

Alice felt how she had imagined she might feel had she never moved to London and acquired unnecessary tastes. She imagined how she might have it in her to do something for somebody and be content with less. She felt that it would be nice to have a little boy who would fall in love with his mum. Or a little girl with hair that needed brushing. She felt that it would be nice to fall in unconditional love with your own creation and think outside yourself, and that this would make for a simpler, nicer life. It was a strange feeling, looking out to sea, and it made Alice wonder – feebly, loosely, and in a style quick to pass – if any fashion could hold up against the sky.

Chris took her hand and with lowered eyes they continued walking. The father caught the ball and threw it to the little boy who gigglingly threw it back out into the sea. Red cheeks and fun-loving spastic hands.

Margate was potentially full of options but no one was quite sure what to do with them. They stood by the edge of the road and discussed how much colder it was than they had anticipated. Suddenly a boy in a tracksuit grabbed Alice by the arm and pushed his face up close to hers –

'Your mum's a slag,' he snarled, and then burst out laughing when Alice blushed. This was the problem with the provinces, she told herself, with the provincial primitives. Distant city folk romanticised them into something other and then desired to keep them so.

The boy ran off. Further up the road he turned round sneering and stuck two fingers up at them –

'You look like dick heads!"

Then ran off again.

Chris had bought a bag of pills and a Kodak Fun Camera – one of those where the film was included and meant for one use only – to record the event, but so far the fun remained abstract. The three used up pictures had all been individual portraits in the Fiesta. Alice took one of Chris by the Cornetto kiosk, and then one of John pointing. Chris took one of Alice running down the beach. They walked in towards the town. *There are no donkeys* Alice thought, slightly wistful, and she had set her heart on bunting. *I gave my heart to cunting bunting. To cunting bunting?*

'The bunting's cunting,' said Alice, and the laughter crept up. It was strange; she was quite a sad person really, and yet she just loved to laugh.

They walked towards a brown brick shopping centre that looked out to sea. DREAMLANDS – written down one side in egg yellow plastic – not a shopping centre, she realised, getting closer, but an amusement arcade. It was a building from a period that still had rationing and where fun was always out of season. *Where was the candyfloss? The beautiful carousel of white and gold horses? The shops selling rock and the Music Hall songs at the end of the pier?* They should have been braver and gone to Cornwall. Dreamlands was the thug-loving dream of one with very little, of teenage truancy and joyrides. Of white skin reflected in the slot machines. It would photograph badly and always look cheap. They should have gone to Cornwall and dropped acid at the Eden Project, but they couldn't afford the petrol.

They walked into Dreamlands. All the amusements were still closed for the winter bar a miniature bowling alley. It was only a pound for forty gos each. They took their Es and waited to come up on them.

'You should have brought Rory,' said Chris, slowly bowling his seventeenth ball of fun. Chris didn't approve of Rory on the grounds that Rory had once bought a magazine called *Achilles' Heel,* for men who felt emasculated by feminism. Chris liked different things – like porn. His favourite film, which he claimed Alice would like too on the grounds of it being "dead glamorous," was set aboard a speed boat. It featured two enhanced women who, in Chris' words, 'bothered each other,' until the swarthy Captain valiantly stepped in and 'sorted everybody out.' Being unimpressed by technology, being overwhelmed by the group aesthetic, Alice chose to remain ignorant. In fact, Alice wasn't even sure if she'd ever actually seen a pornographic film. She *had* once seen a foreign film with an erection in it, but, as it had been ordered through the Guardian website, wasn't sure if it really counted. It was confusing, this art and filth illogicality, and knowing where, as a bohemian, one ought to draw the line.

'Yeah, haven't seen him for a bit,' said John. John liked Rory. John liked everybody. Everybody liked John. 'Shame, decent bloke.'

'We're not together anymore.'

She wasn't even sure if they had ever really been together, but now they definitely weren't. She suspected she was fairly replaceable – appropriate interests, timing.

'Shame,' said John again, and gave her hand a brotherly squeeze, 'decent bloke.'

The bowling became increasingly slow, and Alice felt herself to be a tranquil stone. She was so relieved not to be seeing Rory anymore. It had been only for the afterwards, she decided, the brief normality of sperm stained Marks and Spencer's knickers that had kept it going. For a short and avoided while. And yet he was kind. He was good-looking. Inoffensive. Rory Brown's perfectly nice and normal, maybe even slightly larger than the average, cock – ideally she would have worn gloves...

Chris bought them all a can of Fanta, and used up the Fun Camera on identical blurred shots of the bowling alley. Chris was a conceptualist. He had had an exhibition shortly after graduating that consisted of blurred photographs and coal. It had been well received, but made no money and courted little controversy. It was, he said, about production. Then he had had enough for a bit.

'Are you seeing anyone Chris?' said John, slowly, amused by his own question. They were both holding both hands now. Alice kept smiling because laughing or changing was too energetic. The corners of her mouth ached. She would sleep for days to come. A tranquil stone and then, come the middle of the week, a very black Wednesday.

Chris *was* seeing someone. He was always seeing someone, and always sleeping with whoever else could be insulted into bed on the side. This totalled quite a lot. The standard varied but Chris was a conceptualist. Chris said that one day he would get married, and then he wouldn't cheat anymore because that woman would be his wife, and the mother of his child, and nearly, but not quite, as important as his own mother. Chris loved his mother in the same helpless way that he loved John and tried hard to believe in the security of an established order. Really he was soft, he said. He would marry a good looking girl who knew a bit about art but maybe wasn't an artist and didn't get around. He said. But not for a bit. For some reason he thought she might be French.

John surveyed him critically. 'Do you know what people say about you?' he said.

'What?' It had made Chris edgy.

'Anything with a spine,' said John, and creased up with laughter.

Identical blurred shots and Alice's face ached. Often when she tried to dissect her friends, she was surprised to arrive, not so much at a critique of their stupidity, as a defence of her own masochism. At other times she worried that she might understand more about it than they did. Sometimes

Alice worried that she might be a genius, and for this reason it was important to achieve very little and leave no proof. She touched Chris' hair and smiled. She felt her eyes roll back in her head and Chris put his arms round her and stroke her hair. *What a big baby* she thought. *What a big big baby I am...*

'What are you doing?' said John.

'Giving her a cuddle, alright?' said Chris, he held her with both arms now and gently rocked her. 'Look at her, she's fucked, she needs a cuddle.'

'What sort of cuddle,' said John, with more harsh laughter. 'What sort of cuddle are you planning on sorting her out with then Chris? An anal cuddle?' And manovered Alice so as to take back her hand.

They sat that way indefinitely. Chris's arm around Alice. Alice's hand in John's. There were balls and balls of fun waiting to be bowled in a brown brick and eggy yellow building. Euro-pop re-mixes sounded tinnily in the background. Alice squeezed John's hand and hummed along to the euro-pop.

'I only bought one tape,' said Chris.

John suggested they go and sit on the beach again. They set off with small and ill-thought out steps. It was two o'clock on a windy April afternoon, and suddenly Margate seemed overwhelmingly great. John and Chris became animated. They discussed art in the usual way – Chris would make another piece, about oil this time, John would write about it – and then remembered that the beach was cold. They were at the seaside. It was colder than they had anticipated. Unheated and primitive. A few hundred yards away was a café selling fish and chips. Chris's work would be controversial *and* aggressive. John would write about it. Let's discuss it over chips. They must all set off. It was the only possible action but –

'I am a tranquil stone,' said Alice, not without effort, and felt her words to be lost on the wind. She pulled herself up and reached for both their hands. Dragged by greater strength, fearless, caught up and blown along like the little boy's football, it was delicious for thirty seconds, and then a pebble, heavy again and heavier.

Eternity passed and they reached the café. More grim Fantas and fish and chips no one had the appetite for. Again they sat indefinitely. Held hands. Moved slowly. Mucky – that was the word. They smiled at each other with dry, aching smiles, and gave into the dirty fun of it all. Drank the cheap pop and ignored the sea. How much longer could it last? This precarious beauty for which, they say, the gods are envious? They moved chips around their plates and looked back out to Dreamlands. Twenty-six blurred shots in a bowling alley, and all the official fun was already gone.

Eternity continued passing, and the waitress began to shift from one foot to the other. Chris had absent-mindedly squished three chips into the funnel of the salt pot. John's mushy peas glopped onto the table. They must all set off again. It was the only possible action again. But where to now? The beach was cold and the sea was relentless. Back to Dreamlands? Or the car? Again eternity passed. Indefinite sitting. Chris might use the Fun Camera for *his* next show. He would take twenty-six blurred shots of the sea with the Fun Camera and then pour oil *on* the photographs. It would be about production, but abstract. He could put a bird *in* the oil. It would be controversial *and* aggressive, and again eternity passed.

Chris was elated. He had found what he needed. John was elated too – he understood. They were wrecked and united, and set off again.

They had forgotten that there were some beers left in the car, so, avoiding the outside, they found a pub and ordered some more. A pub with a neatly framed view of the car and the café and the sea, panelled in dark brown imitation wood, and with a jukebox playing Fleetwood Mac:

If I could maybe I'd give you my world
But how can I when you won't take it from me?

Alice tapped her toe and hummed along. She loved Fleetwood Mac, although now she tried hard to like other, more sophisticated things, more. It was the way they really *meant* it, while still adhering to a heartstring playing formula that had proved so very moving. The completely sincere Rumours cover, where Stevie Nicks danced in a homemade ballet outfit and tossed her fluffy hair – how could anyone fail to be touched? Allegedly, Stevie's septum had rotted away through drug use, and later on she had had to hire someone to blow the coke up her arse instead. *Poor sad Stevie.* It was a cream and brown cover with a Seventies folk-esque typeface that, in spite of seeing it many times, Alice had never owned. Secretly she preferred to buy Best Ofs rather than individual albums, as that way you got all the real hits.

'I only bought one tape and it's in the car,' said Chris, watching Alice, concerned by an unbridgeable gulf of inner predilection.

'Why d'you bring *Aladdin Sane*?' she said, and gave him a giggling pinch, '*Hunky Dory's* so much better.'

The boys put fifty pee down to be next up for the snooker. The song ended, changed. The break - break - break as the sea hits the rocks.

She could see the sea from the pub window. A cold steel line of water against a cold steel line of sand. She sipped her lager and reached for John's hand. Rarely was she so openly affectionate. Rarely unafraid to acknowledge that her happiness might be linked to another's. Another wave of calm washed over her. She sipped her lager and closed her eyes in order to block out the sea. She saw the image of herself running down the beach in soft focus, black and white: an existential heroine with a great Joan of Arc bob. She pictured the gun in her hand and laughed. Nice place to kill an Arab. She choked on a mouthful of beer.

'I've got some speed,' said Chris.

'What?'

The drug of choice for suburban teens. Reebok classics and Elizabeth

Duke. The papers said there was a plan to turn Blackpool into the new Las Vegas. Eventually they might reach Margate and, well, once it reached a certain point, best to just go with it.

'Alright then just a bit.' And still happy, but lighter.

They sat in the dark little pub, all swirly patterned carpet and saucy seaside postcards pinned up behind the bar.

'I hate Hogarth,' said Alice happily. Now lighter.

'Hogarth is due for a resurgence,' said John. 'He was a great satirist.'

'He was a great ad man,' added Chris. 'Every time he completed a painting he put an advert in the paper for the engraved copies. Then, when he realised how much that was making him, he started doing sets at half the size, so more and more people could get in on the Hogarth brand. He was making political marketing moves that were way ahead of his time. Great ad-man.' He said again.

'I'm an artist, so I prefer Fragonard,' said Alice.

'Fragonard's for pussies,' said Chris, and spat his gum on the floor.

'I don't care much for Fragonard either,' said John, in the tone of someone wiser, and ran his hand across his manly scalp.

John suggested they walk along the beach again. They had, after all, come for a day out by the sea. They walked faster now, ran occasionally, in the half-light. Three in a gang, silhouetted against the sky. Chris, who was still carrying his pint glass from the pub, threw it, and beer and glass sloshed randomly through the air. They all collapsed with weak hysteria. Cold wet grit of sand in Alice's shoes and pockets, and stinging wind. She had tripped and fallen and lay eyes shut and smiling near the sea. Her heart beating fast but still somehow calm, and she thought: this is bliss. It really was. A simulated experience some might say. A substitute. But a substitute for what?

Another, lesser, experience? Greasy fingers and damp waves of euphoria. In the closing of an eyelid – bliss. A light smattering of rain fell on her face. Alice laughed silently and weakly. Flapped her arms up and down and made an angel in the sand.

'I don't know what to do to be happy.' It was Chris, lying beside her, one stage more gone. He was disorientated and keen to inflict his indecision. 'I'm not happy. I can't be happy.' His lip trembled.

'Why not pour oil over some birds,' she said, and her laughter was unstoppable. 'Why not burn ants with a magnifying glass or pull the legs off a spider.'

It might be nice one day to have a little boy. Chris was atrocious and selfish, but then so was she and it felt like a connection. They were both laughing now. Alice climbed over him; one hand briefly touched his stomach, and made an angel on the other side. John tried to take a picture with the Fun Camera not realising all the film was gone. And yet they were still having fun! *Such a poor poor boy,* thought Alice, and took Chris's hand in hers:

'Now come on move your arms.'

She made him move his arms up and down until he made a third angel and kept on laughing about the oily bird. That was a silly idea. His hair had dye and gunk and salt in it, it clung to his head like moss to a rock, and she could make out the faint traces of teen acne. Sometimes he was incredibly beautiful.

John lay down to make a fourth angel. Alice reached for his hand too so he didn't feel left out. Then they all stayed lying by the sea and looked at the marks their bodies had made. They were so fucked. Dreamland's edges blurred into the night, but the yellow letters still made shapes in the darkness.

They lay that way indefinitely again, and then with relief walked back along the beach. They were still high. It was dark. They got back in the car. John tried several times to put the key in the ignition but kept missing. Eventually he got there and pulled the car out into the darkness. He kept bumping into things and laughing. So did Alice. She lay on the back seat and kicked off her shoes. Then she placed her feet against the window. Chris put Bowie back on, and Alice hummed. They had only brought one tape. John got settled and drove more smoothly. More beers opened, and the night seeped into day.

It's a crash course for the ravers / It's a drive in Saturday... They were young, they were beautiful. David Bowie plays along a darkened road. Anticipation - but then nothingness, and the perfection of.

Part 3

Hackney Wick III

Sunday evening was bleak and in the manner of comedowns. They watched *La Haine*. The lead character, Vince, stared at his reflection and asked, *C'est a moi tu parles? C'est a moi tu parles?* An actor pretending to be a poor boy pretending to be Robert De Niro pretending to be a lunatic. Already it was too familiar. There were a few seconds of poetry – a window on the Paris high rise was opened and the voice of Edith Piaf soared mournfully out – but on the whole irritation was not lessened through the use of black and white. The stupidity of poor boys.

Alice felt the strain of subtitles pinprick behind her eyes. She must waste no more time and make an entirely new set of unrelated friends. All her friends were horrific. Everyone else was boring. But often her friends were boring. But often they were horrific. Tiredness stabbed brutally until bile seeped out. The warehouse was cold and squalid. The people next door had seen rats by the bins. And John was tidying and baking. And Chris was sitting on the couch playing with the remote. And Alice filled up with righteous anger as inside, and all around her, the stupidity escalated.

All the dirty pots and pans, of which there were many, were being stacked and piled up by John without actually ever being cleaned. Why didn't he clean them? He turned on taps, left them on, and then forgot about them as another bit of pseudo-tidying caught his eye. He kneaded dough. He scattered flour. John was making bread, and it was needlessly manic. None of them had been to sleep yet, but John had just received a text message from a girl he liked and arranged to go round to hers for dinner tomorrow night. With bread. A sensitive man, a cultured bachelor who cooked in the style of, scattered flour and allowed chaos to reach new heights through a masquerade of civilised behaviour. He even whistled slightly under his breath.

And Alice pictured a future John, needing dough, whistling slightly under his breath, laughing with his lovely wife and lovely baby as he recalled those heady single days. He'd tell her how they'd wound up in a tacky bit of Kent, how nothing had been open, how they'd got a bit fucked, and then she'd laugh her lovely laugh at him for being just so crazy. John was a constant. Alice pictured John then as he was now. Such a man and such a boy. Pictured how his lovely wife would turn off the taps, wash the pots, laugh at him lovingly as he laughed back...

And Alice, brittle, unloving, aware of the taps and sat on the couch, felt a further surge of annoyance. Why was John never tired? Why were the pots not washed? And then instant guilt because John was so kind and good while she was bitter, tired and bitter. She turned away from John and looked at Chris instead. He was trying to prise the back off the remote control. He wanted the battery for something else. The old battery was unlikely to be replaced afterward, and they would have to get off the couch to change channels as a result.

Chris finally removed the plastic backing and dropped it on the floor. It fell onto a slashed open box of videos, one of which ('LEATHERSEX

– Nymphomaniacs are trapped in a meat factory and pumped') had been removed. He looked content. And suddenly she was weary of their idealised crusade, suffocated by an open-plan listlessness.

It was so stale as to be unbearable and yet no alternative presented itself.

Alice knew that they were spoilt brats who wilfully suspended disbelief and, through use of the word 'artist', considered their sensitivity more than a middle-class conceit. She read the papers occasionally, and there was torture and terrorism and bigger things at stake. Issues in faraway lands that photographed so wonderfully as to become unreal – the Taliban burning columns of video cassettes under a bright and foreign sun, a crying child with a gun held to its head, and other cinematic triggers. People existed who couldn't afford to buy in on nihilistic feelings – a bourgeois merchandise – and with whom she had nothing in common beyond the endorsement of an image.

There was a large crash. Pots fell in a clatter onto the concrete floor. Chris and Alice turned to look. John looked back at them, then at the plates, then back at them again, uncertain. Slowly he picked everything up off the floor and piled it in the same insecure place at the edge of the table. Relief soothed his features, and a little more flour was calmly sprinkled. John smiled and resumed whistling slightly under his breath. Chris turned back to the TV, and sometimes a copy of the Futurist Manifesto.

Looking over Chris' shoulder she read point three – *Literature has up to now magnified pensive immobility, ecstasy and slumber* – but the Futurists weren't futuristic, they were nearly ninety years ago now, and therefore out of date.

And thought swirled miserably back on itself

Loathful. Sloth like. Sick.

C'est a moi tu parles? C'est a moi tu parles?

The video was re-wound and played back for what felt like the hundredth time, but was maybe only the tenth. And Chris was content with his focused arrogance. And John continued to bake. Zippity zapperty, onwards and upwards, they all raced further ahead. *I know more*, thought Alice. *I want more*. But where did that get her, a bag of wet cement, a bit-player in someone else's film?

C'est a moi tu parles?

'Hey, I've heard back from that gallery!' They had set off before yesterday's post arrived, and the austere manila envelope, already a mess of shreds, had only just caught Chris' eye, 'But it's all good.'

He was smiling with childish excitement and pushing random buttons on the now defunct remote control. Torn pieces of envelope fell on LEATHERSEX and littered the floor.

'What gallery? What?'

'That gallery from ages ago that said they liked my photographs. Well I sent them my portfolio and now they want to make me a star.' He pressed the buttons faster, 'Well, put me in a show,' he conceded, and kicked Alice softly in the leg.

'That's great' said John from the dough, 'Congratulations mate, well done.'

Chris stared hard at Alice who had yet to respond. She decided not to put out because it wasn't fair. Instead she pressed her lips together so that they made a hard tight line. She resented the way he sat on the couch, lazy and Neoclassical, historic and histrionic, letting things fall in his lap and then considering it deserved. Chris was a drama queen who heard the shovel hit the ground whenever a parental handout was not forthcoming and now this - dead birds, oil and universal adoration. She was a resentful person who resented. The Taliban were burning videos! Soon they would burn DVDs! For pity's sake it wasn't fair.

C'est a moi tu parles?

There were no reasons. It was just like that. You weren't good for having less, for being the victim. You were good for doing a good thing. And sometimes God stood up for bastards while lazy people lazed. Plates crashed and planes crashed, a column of video cassettes caught fire under a blazing foreign sun, and the television blared. Alice Grisham sighed, surveyed a dubious stain, and felt herself to be removed from life.

The Freud Museum

Armond was waiting by the tube near the Freud Museum at precisely one o'clock. Armond was precise. And particular with his tastes. He was head of the Grade A-Gays, which meant he *always* wore Chanel Platinum Egoiste and sometimes bought socks by Falke.

In a trait common to both homosexuals and psychopaths Armond viewed the appearance of women with a strip-light gaze. He immediately acknowledged the chipped nail on Alice's right hand through a barely perceptible but also incredibly debasing little jerk on the upper-left lip, and delivered the reproof as someone made invincible through money. And Armond was indeed very, very wealthy. Victim to the endless amusements of private means – culture, crack, group-sex in blacked-out rooms – a literary debauchery that intrigued Alice and sailed the friendship on through waves of repugnance. It was not as though Armond were entirely bad, after all, just ruined and deluded in the manner of Caligula. It was not as though Alice was innocent either, just currently lacking direction and funds.

And already each leafy Hampstead step since the tube had placed a plastic spoon firmly in her mouth, clarified that she was not rich and not from London – and yet it afforded a strange delight, to be outside looking in. Kids, up in the city on a cheap day return. Nights at the circus. It was so distant as to be unenviable – a through-the-looking-glass image of known yet crooked spectacle that drew you in like so many magazines. Alice watched the Lion Tamer place his head between the lion's jaws and felt a voyeuristic thrill. To be sat so far away left you free only to admire the performance, involvement being the view from a much closer seat.

She shared this thought with Armond, who agreed out of the side of his mouth. Armond considered it tasteful to appear unassuming. The sentiment was pretty, this he appreciated, but as the owner of a private box, soon lost upon the wind. To a man of the world, Alice was an amusing child and little more. A very common kind of butterfly, self indulgent and grandiose, who fluttered by every four weeks or so and just missed being suffocated in the collector's jar. *I won't have my wings pinned,* thought Alice, and the fear pumped a surge of adrenaline.

Upon reaching the house they both paused before the mutual territory of the unknown. *And surely any kind of butterfly can brighten the sky, lessen the tedium,* thought Alice, *any... any* movement *even.* Just the simple act of paying the entrance fee – of throwing a pebble in a puddle to watch the ripples spread – was enough of a reason for working up excitement:

Roll up! Roll up! For The Freud Museum! All inclusive. Never previously visited. A fantastic opportunity to Look-In-Side. One afternoon only, for two pounds only. A wonderful experience but Not-for-Everybody. Thank you very much, sir, madam. Roll up! Roll up! ...

'Sometimes,' Armond was telling her, 'I have a reoccurring dream about the Strong Wolf. I'm walking in a desert full of elephants. I know that they could trample on me, but I'm not afraid because I also know that I'm protected. Every time one of the elephants gets too close the Strong Wolf appears and carries it off in its mouth.'

They were inside the museum. It smelt fusty.

'Aren't the elephants a lot bigger than the Strong Wolf?' she was both curious about this literal difference in size, and pleased that the circus theme continued. Alice liked a theme. It was close to a structure but not intimidatingly so. She saw how the audience would gasp while the beautiful lady daringly lay down beneath the elephant's raised leg. Saw a dozen white horses and spangley leotards and horses, horses, horses and felt wonderfully near to madness. They must have a party with a circus theme. They must have one *soon*.

'But doesn't it matter? This difference in scale?' she asked.

'No it doesn't matter because it's the *Strong* Wolf. It's my reoccurring dream. Don't you have any reoccurring dreams?'

'Only the usual type. My teeth fall out. I'm somewhere important without my clothes on. I try to run but – '

'Oh. Oh dear. Doesn't anything nice ever happen?' This subconscious failure to shine disappointed him. Her dreams were passé.

'Well sometimes I get rescued.' It was true. Sometimes she did.

'Rescued? Who by?' He was interested now. Projecting a generosity of interest in Alice. Sly and sideways like a side-winding snake. A coiled up side-winding snake waiting for the thing he would choose to venomously remember and bring up at a later date.

'Well by a – ' Alice faltered. It was a dangerous admission. 'By a man. A man in a Volvo.'

Again a sideways look but Armand stayed silent, saving it all up. They were stood by Freud's couch, which to Alice's mind looked rather comfortable.

Above it hung a painting of the Sphinx. Opposite, a glass cabinet filled with ancient looking artefacts, unearthed from deep within, and turned to face the couch with a symbolism that was crushing. On the way downstairs they had passed a portrait of Freud smoking a cigar. This was placed next to an ashtray with a half smoked cigar in it. Probably not Freud's. Alice yawned.

'Sometimes a cigar is just a cigar,' she said.
'Who said that?'
'Freud.'

Freud spent only the last year of his life in Hampstead, a haven from the Nazis. But all his things from Vienna – from the cushions, to the curtains, to the crockery – had been brought along and rearranged exactly as they had always been, and so the reconstruction of another, foreign life had become the definitive one.

And Alice imagined Hackney Wick seventy years hence. First it would go through a forgotten period, obviously, as they all moved on to other things, lowered the standard of their dreaming and accepted the real – where they would remain known only to themselves. But then, later, it would be filled with solemn art historians trying to rebuild the filth where they, the now famous artists, had once lived. Gradually they would piece together an accurate picture aided by several films of Fun Camera and a few party Polaroids. A young academic would be forced to masturbate onto a plate of beans in order to create the most faithful reconstruction possible... A lab based mixture of Vivienne Westwood's *Libertine* and excrement would be rubbed into the bathroom tiles... An image of John holding a Cornetto and pointing would be held up to the light - 'This was how they enjoyed themselves then.'

Back upstairs a black and white video of the Museum played. There was a grainy photograph on the screen of Freud's couch, over which hung a painting of the Sphinx, ancient looking artefacts, etc.

'This' said the voice-over, 'Was the room in which psychoanalysis took place.'

'I don't believe in the unconscious,' said Alice, over the voice-over, 'It's out of date. That's the view in current thinking. That actually there is no unconscious and that Freud is very dusty.'

It was true. She had read about it only days earlier. She had discussed it with John. It was the current view. It was Informed.

'Oh really?' Armond's laugh came out the tiniest corner. He had taken, Alice noticed, to parting his hair very far on the one side. Like Hitler. 'Oh well then, I don't think I want to believe in Trafalgar Square.'

They walked back down the stairs and Armond put the half-smoked cigar in his pocket. They sniggered.

'Sometimes the criminal wants to be caught,' said Alice.

'Who said that? Freud?'

'Yes!'

She jumped the last two steps and Armond laughed, not unpleasantly, at her. Alice would have liked to ask him to jump down the stairs too. Then they could have run to the top and begun again. Then another time. She didn't ask because he would have said no.

They went back to the couch, and Alice thought again that it looked inviting. It was heaped with soft cushions and heavy Indian rugs. Not so much a safe place for problems, as a safe place generally - one where you could crawl in, shut your eyes and have a really nice nap. Maybe a Horlicks... And yet at the same time there was something almost depraved about the study, with its old leather odour, antiques and curios. The intense clutter of value and a couch designed to lie back and sink into. Spiritualism, occultism and other turn of the century fads – psychoanalysis seemed profligate. Rich, jaded voices haunted the couch, said listen, listen, listen to me. *Did Freud really listen?* thought Alice, *or did he just want his audience to be comfortable?*

No unconscious might well be wishful thinking, but it was a dream to save expenditure, the point to an inner life surely being its very lack of existence.

The point being lack.

Armond caught the eye of an old lady. Briefly he took his dick out of his trousers and wiggled his tongue at her. The woman, quite possibly someone's grandmother, quite possibly a person who had produced a brand new person from deep inside her own cunt, pretended to be shocked by the homosexual's flaccid penis. Armond cackled loudly and without amusement, and for that split second Alice was sure his mouth had housed a black, forked tongue. A moment later he was sombre again, staring passively at a statue in a cabinet as though completely oblivious to the scene, while the woman left the room making a choked tutting sort of noise.

Alice yawned for the second time, she wondered about Freud, and whether he hadn't taken it all a bit far.

There was no tearoom and the Museum's gift shop proved unexciting. An eraser and a double-ended pen were the best it had to offer. The assistant eyed them suspiciously and then returned to his book. Alice looked anxiously at the merchandise. It was disappointing not to make a purchase. Eventually Armond gave in and bought an eraser.

'It's not that I'm anti-Freud as such,' said Alice, 'but you know, that whole male ego thing.'

'That whole male ego thing? That's quite a thing to be anti-.'

Armond was examining a second orange eraser, and not concentrating properly on what he or Alice was saying. This may or may not have been the result of cocaine affecting his short-term memory. He did a lot of cocaine. Then again it may have been because he was completely corrupted and had no interests beyond his own immediate desire. His eraser was green. Perhaps the orange one was better? Perhaps he should buy both just in case? One might be better. There was also a blue eraser... He feared so much to be without, that

Alice understood. She decided she would like to find a soothing thing to say and say it.

'Maybe. They're very nice. I didn't know you drove?'

He had thrown down the erasers in fatigued loathing, and taken out a pair of gloves. String backed pigskin in palest beige. Gentlemen's' driving gloves in the exact same shade as his cashmere scarf.

'I don't.'

There was an Italian delicatessen in the direction of Hampstead village that served drinks at the back. Alice had a Mocha with extra cream, Armond a semi-skimmed, decaffeinated Cappuccino. Armond appeared to be dissatisfied with the green eraser. He picked away at it slowly and flicked the strip-light on in her direction.

'That's a hideous brooch,' he said. 'Is it an heirloom?'

It was Gothic Victorian kitsch. Garnet lovebirds set in tarnished silver. It had belonged to one of Alice's various great-Aunts. Now it pinned a black silk scarf to the neck of a black lace blouse. It wasn't quite valuable, and sat against skin a milky, markable pale. Semi-precious. One had hoped to affect a dying swan.

'No' Alice lied, 'Steinberg and Tolkien.'

'Oh? Maybe I like it then.'

Time passed and they had a second coffee. Armond picked away at more of the eraser. Over half was gone. Pastel coloured fragments fell on orange pine. Only Freud's mouth and chin remained intact and minty fresh. The video had explained how, in later life, cancer of the palate had caused his jaws to lock together. The cine-film footage had shown a stern faced Freud, complete with cigar clamped between his static lips. *Poor Freud*, thought Alice. And hoped Mrs Freud had not been put off.

'Could you love someone with a deformity?' she asked.

'How big a deformity? I could probably manage a squint but I wouldn't like to commit to anything more.'

'What about a locked jaw?'

'No. Although saying that I did go to a party where people were having sex with amputees. I quite got off on that to be honest. All the spunky stumps.'

Armond resumed his coffee, for a moment introspective. Alice felt disgusted, but then again why should she be? Provided everyone was consenting of course, provided they stayed on the right side of the bohemian line.

'Did you hear about the party Camilla and Crispin went to in South Kensington?' she said after a while. 'The one with the pillow-cases and the dog in the tent? There was loads of free champagne but they only stayed for half an hour. Crispin said the whole place reeked of AIDS.'

'Really?' said Armond. 'Sounds an absolute dream.'

Alice took this as a cue to expand on her desire for a fourth painting and the resurgence of beauty. Armond listened more carefully for a short period because he was a revolutionary conceptualist who was also interested in beauty, but a conceptual one that could stand up to harsh lighting. He revealed that he was planning to make a subliminal floor piece out of a skirting board. Both had yet to begin, might never begin, and failure stayed hidden in the shadows. *Why had they chosen art,* Alice wondered, *some vague belief in the eternal?*

Armond quickly became bored and returned to his criticism of the brooch, which he might like for being so hideous, but then again might not for the same reason. He continued in this vein until this time it was Alice whose attention drifted. Sensing this, Armond tried to buy her a cake she didn't want by way of compensation. It was how it always was.

Could people still believe in the eternal? she wondered, *the creation of an enduring image?* She watched as Armond rediscovered the stolen cigar in his pocket, dropped it absently onto the floor and then ground it beneath his heel.

'Do you think we're special for being artists?' she said.

'No. I think we're *marginally* more interesting than some people on the basis of our not being stupid. But only *marginally*.'

He pulled angrily at the last bit of eraser that would not tear. Gave up and threw it in the ashtray.

'I am continually robbed of my illusions,' said Alice.

All of the eraser was now in pieces and Armond looked appalled. The tabletop was untidy in an unclean way, creating an imprecise disorder which contradicted the day's tone. They moved over to the next table that the waitress had just wiped clean. They both smirked, aware of the ridiculous fussiness they created for themselves. Alice spilt a little coffee during the transition. On the second table. They looked towards a third table but that would suggest an effort bordering on madness.

'Do you think art actually matters?' Alice said, with something that to her was nearly aggression and at another point in another life might have been. 'Do you know anyone who actually cares about more than saying they've been in something with someone, and it got two lines in Time-Out? Who looks at a picture and sees a picture and not a short hand for commercial success? I saw Nicki and Sam in the Tate a while back and it was all I could do to keep from screaming.'

'No, not really no. But art's an occupation, and that's already enough.'

'No it's not enough,' said Alice, and surprised herself by realising both that she meant it and clung onto her faith in it with terrified, clawing hands, 'because I'd rather be a bad poet than a good business man and that's all there is to hang onto!'

But already it was enough when the day was so pleasant and they did so little. Coffee, companionship and the museum - most of the day was already gone, dissolved into a soluble sugar solution of living, and all of it had been necessary. She thought of Freud's couch and again felt sleepy. Where was the room for anything more? Where was the space for art in the immense labour of existence?

'Nicki and Sam *together*?' said Armond after a moment. 'Nicki and Sam *both at once*? I would have screamed at those evil, grabbing tarts.'

A silence fell between them. They both faced the horror for a second and then there was nothing more to do.

'What lovely cufflinks,' said Alice with equal feeling and re-pinned her brooch, slightly higher and to the left.

Interview

It was her absolute best and most expensive thing. Plumes of feathers, beading, velvet ribbon and a veil. No fruit or animals. It was a hat. Perhaps, Alice suspected, an inappropriate hat, but they were at a point where to remove it would only create further problems. Instead, she cultivated an expression of absolute blankness, having come to believe that in moments of crisis this was often the best response.

'So how do you think your work will benefit from the time in Italy?'

The woman doing the asking presented herself as one in a retro sense. Long grey hair and wooden beads. A woman, a mother, an artist - she was the sort to address herself as such and not shave her armpits as a fashion statement. You could tell from the beads. Her look looked into Alice with a curious disdain, at odds with an opposing type of illusion. She pursed her dry lips and ran the wooden beads condescendingly between her dry fingers. She returned Alice's look with an equal, but unkind, blankness.

They were eight minutes into an interview marked by the awkward pause. An exchange of ill-timed looks and clashing sentences, where the politeness jarred. At no point had Alice considered the questions she might be asked. The slides had been meticulously Photoshopped and saved on a borrowed laptop. Her clothes were expensive and took on a, she believed, European tone. These interrogations were consequently a dull and superfluous means of intimidation, and one that she would rise above. The room was cold. The lighting industrial. And a woman set herself against a brightly feathered bird. It was not so much that Alice felt out of her depth – rather that she was too far up the pool to be seen from the shallow end.

'Well,' Alice's Nars reddened lips parted beneath an expanse of black net. She had barely eaten in a week to cover the cost of a lipstick and felt the added weight to her sentences. 'Well. I consider myself a Romantic. I am a great fan of Fellini, though lately his cinematic representations have begun to bore me. I have asked myself why this is. The answer? I am now ready for Rome itself.'

It was a statement delivered with poise and timing that came out as it would on the page. Bureaucracy went for Alice, and in her defence a paragraph. She was surprised by the silence. Then by her surprise. Shuffled papers. It was an intimidating draft of a room, flaking and establishment. Sallow academics breathed in and out a papery air. A strip-light flickered. A further silence.

Alice shivered slightly and drew a white mink stole around her shoulders. She was wearing a large faux-diamond ring *on top* of her black gloves. Her gaze stayed on the gloves. Reassuring. Obviously it was unable to stay on the hat.

'The thing is, we like your, errr, paintings, however, to be honest, there doesn't seem to be that many of them. The scholarship is awarded on the premise that the Rome artist will use their time abroad, errr, productively. Were we to offer you this award, we would need to feel assured of your producing work of a consistent quality and, errr, quantity.'

She was annoying, this woman, who delivered every statement with the smug irony and lowered eyelids of one corrupted by jurisdiction. She had got herself up in a way that was ugly and proud. That said 'I am a strong woman, artist, mother,' and expected respect. It was too easily satisfied with itself, this way of thinking. *She is annoying,* thought Alice and tugged at a gloved finger. She understood herself to be magnificent, arrogant, young – and ready to be killed by a camera phone. She was wearing a hat with a veil!

'Yes.' She crossed her new Jonathan Aston seemed-stockings, and a pointed patent flat gave out a satisfying click. 'I am working on a fourth painting.'

There didn't seem anything else to say really. She recalled an old black and white film that she had seen as a teenager, the title escaped her, in which Marlene Dietrich is found out as a spy and sentenced to death. When finally faced with the firing squad and believing herself about to die, she calmly removes her hat and lights a cigarette. Alice reached inside her handbag and emerged with a gold filter Sobraine, because some of the old things - like Marlene Dietrich, late night on channel four – were still okay to like, and still seemed to belong to you alone.

Just like what you like. It's okay. Just like what you like.

Alice drew back the veil, found her lighter, lit up and inhaled deeply.

'I'm sorry but we have a no smoking policy.'

Alice put out her cigarette. She wasn't a smoker anyway. A dark red circle marked the paper and inferred profligacy cut short. *She is annoying*, thought Alice, and let her lip curl just enough. Exhibit A returned to the depths of the Fifties mini-clutch.

'Perhaps you could talk us through some of your work and tell us about your creative process?'

'Yes.'

Alice gave up and clicked the mouse onto the first picture of the first painting, which was projected large, and surprisingly bright, on the wall opposite. It wasn't a bad painting now John had neatened it up a bit. It wasn't bad at all. Alice reminded herself that she had academic tendencies and a photographic memory when she concentrated. That she had a first class honours degree in style over content. And that she could hold on to that and talk the talk. She touched the ring again, felt reassured and was ready. She straightened her shoulders, adjusted the angle of the hat, and began:

'I,' said Alice Grisham, black lashes raised towards the heavens, marble skin luminous beneath the gauze, 'believe in beauty. Within the context of art, it can be transcendental.'

Her skin was pale and clear. She lisped slightly but she was young, you liked it or you didn't. She lisped slightly but she believed in beauty, swore to it on a stack of bibles, but felt somehow that the jury was against her. She was young, a believer, who knew what she liked. And if you liked beauty, in a painting, in a moment, well what was wrong with that? With that beautiful idea? Wasn't it enough to be beautiful?

Oh! Reader! Don't hate her for being beautiful!

'Within the context of *art?*'

There were six of them in all. Four men and two women. Mid-forties and up. Both women did not look like the kind of women who would wear hats. They wore wooden beads and natural fibres. You could tell from the natural fibres. The men were men who never had adolescence, and were suspicious of charm. Born exactly as they were now and at long last achieving a social norm through published papers, they had reached an age where they were expected to be out of touch and revelled in it. And, with this, a revenge – power wielded over those they had never been – feigned indifference to a pretty bird in a hat.

'Yes. In an art context. I usually explain a painting in terms of how it summarises the beauty or anguish in my own life,' said Alice, 'and then use this summary as a fast track to emotion. But that's a lazy way to put it. If I'm completely honest, then I have to admit that that's only a small part. For me, a successful picture doesn't so much refine the reality, as perpetually exceed it. And this... this... *transcendental* escape from my life, or my self even, I mean, well, it's close to spiritual.'

Nine slides of three paintings was not enough of a scam. Neither was the outfit. She began to talk mechanically about history and theory. Clicking between the slides, flitting between known ideas. Agreeing with known ideas, accepting and reaffirming them. She had academic tendencies, but six sallow people would ultimately be responsible for a life changing experience. Fate rested on the shoulders of six people who failed, refused even, to understand the semiotics of a hat.

Hope burned and faded. She talked up the talk, and moths fluttered in her chest. She talked insipid learning, with words that fluttered and singed against an overheated rib cage. Young and arrogant and knowing what it was to want.

The panel were somewhat more interested. *Somewhat.*

And all the while conscious of an ugly, overriding aim to please, as one dusty moth wing caught light then another then another – a dark and cloying heat. It rose in a panic of wanting too much. She would wear a Laura Ashley dress in Rome. When she came back she would wear black and gold sunglasses –

'I've never lived abroad,' said Alice with exasperation, 'I think I would be different there. More likable. The light, you see, will be brighter.'

'What?'

'The light. The light will be... it will be... Oh, oh, I'm sorry,' said Alice, a bird banging into the glass.

'What?'

'I'm sorry. It doesn't come across. I'm disgusted myself.'

It was unnecessary. Shameful. A dull silent blanket fell over her. Dry air. Shaken hands. A little boat sailed perilously near the edge of the world and someone took a digital picture.

The interview ground to a halt and a veiled lady walked out into the afternoon.

The Sir John Soane Museum

Sir John Soane (1753-1837) opened his home to the general public as a museum that 'amateurs and students' might visit, whilst still alive. He was an architect famed for his taste, vision and humour and, being the son of a humble bricklayer, keen to share the fruits of his labour with the working man. He stayed true to the streets, threw open the doors of his home and castle, and scattered a cultural largesse – Sir John Soane said that the kids were alright.

The museum housed his collections. They were all on different themes. There was the basement filled with Neoclassical sculpture for instance, the room of too many paintings with its salon-style hang, and the satirical cubbyhole built for the ghost of an imaginary monk (a reference to the leisured classes and their poor but expensive taste for a rather kitsch kind of Gothic, made manifest through the building of follies, employing of faux-hermits, reading of Byron, and the like) above all however, it was the palace of an eccentric unafraid to indulge his whims and, as the years passed, a monument to a historic accumulator.

To the right upon entering, Soane had created a very red room with circular, convex mirrors hung in the corners. At the time the house was built, it was fashionable to take these items to the countryside. When one found a pleasing, but possibly overwhelming view of nature, they would turn their back on the windswept reality in order to look at the smaller (safer?) other-way-round version in the mirror. A fancy Sir John, being original, brought back inside his own house so that one charming quirk might frame another and thus gracefully distort the domestic. Alice and Camilla were stood there now. It was known as the picturesque period.

'I'm considering a new dress for it,' said Camilla looking up into a mirrored circle, 'but perhaps should invest in a coat.' She had reached a point in life where she invested. It signified a move towards realism – both a contentment and acceptance.

'Will it still have a Russian theme? Black fur and white snow? Is there an Opera set in Russia?' asked Alice, who had been known to impulse buy.

It was an occasional Sunday that saw them both at a good angle. The party had yet to happen, might happen, might not, but fun lay in the deconstruction of minutiae and the aesthetic pursuit of an ideal.

'It's still Russian, and if I buy a dress it'll be extravagant. Maybe lilac, like that one Julie Christie wears at the start of *Dr Zhivago*. Or maybe like that one but green. Something with a cold look anyway.'

'I'm thinking of being extravagant too,' said Alice, suddenly she had decided to invest also, 'but I need to save up a bit first.'

The room had been coloured-in in a dramatic style. The walls were a deep, affluent, and bloody shade of red with black, white and gold detailing. Alice went to sit down on one of the over-polished, high-backed chairs, but then noticed that each seat was already taken-up with a decorative thistle

– more discreet than a velvet rope or placard warning not to touch, yet, simultaneously tinged with sadism. A marble bust sat in a cove, reflected back and forth between the corners. There were bookshelves and windows and other things you might expect to find in a home. There were John Soane's books on the bookshelves for example; normalities that only accentuated the room's warped scale. The space was not quite large enough for the grandeur at which it aimed, but somehow this added to its charm, afforded its creator a humanity. Alice stood so that looking up one way they were both in profile.

'I'm going to invite Lara and Armond and their lot, and you and your boys and your lot, and some people from college, but not that many – '

De dum de dum de dum. De dum de dum de dum. De dum de dum. De dum de dum –

'Did I tell you I saw Nicki and Sam a while back,' cut in Alice, eager and absent, tapping her toe in accompaniment. 'They're both being highly successful. Two reviews in Time-Out. I meant to tell you at The Wallace Collection but I forgot.'

It was true. She had forgotten. Sometimes it ate her up with jealousy, and sometimes it was so boring it floated off without her realising.

'Nick *and* Sam? Nicki *and* Sam *together*? Oh no', said Camilla, but then, 'their sort of success is lowbrow,' she added reflectively.

Alice ran a gloved finger over a vase. The bust's marble lips sat too high up and out of reach.

'I'm glad we're highbrow,' said Alice.

Camilla smiled. They linked arms and moved to the next room. It was nice to have a friend that understood.

The museum was famous for its Hogarths. Eight paintings in all contributed to *The Rake's Progress*, a series of small oils, painted some thirty years befor Fragonard began his major works. They folded out on boards, only to be seen at certain times and with the assistance of a museum warden, in Sir John's specially designed room for paintings. He built a glass-bottomed walkway where, until her death, his wife had liked to stand and view the works. John (Sir, not to be confused with our) liked to stand below, gazing up through the rustle of her eighteenth century skirts and smiling. Though disappointed by the conduct of his lazy children, Soane was always very proud. Of his collections. Of his wife. He had only opened up the house after she passed away. Until then her adoration had been enough. After that he needed visitors.

Alice did not immediately take to *The Rake's Progress*:

> Tom Rakewell, a silly, selfish boy, corrupted by a windfall – the little-mourned death of his wealthy father – and out of his depth in the fashionable society he now has the means to frequent, gives in, in meticulous detail, to the most spectacular debauchery.
>
> As soon as he's been measured for a new and modish suit, he throws off Sarah Young, the innocent servant girl he has previously seduced, the moral alternative to self-destruction in a potty-mouthed comic strip, and hurries to London, eager for drinking and whores.
>
> Tom soon arrives at the notorious Rose Tavern, where he parties with prostitutes and ne'er-do-wells until the early hours. His jacket becomes stained and unbuttoned as the night progresses, his sword unsheathed. In a weirdly child-like touch, his socks fall down around his ankles and expose a tender glimpse of unmarked skin, while two older women, black patches applied as fashion in an attempt to hide their syphilitic scars, laugh and steal his watch. Tom is unawares, however, the willing victim of an alcoholic stupor, and all those around look-on, pretending not to see.
>
> The party continues – bilious, gloomy and obscured from natural light. More wine is poured. Then spilled. More laughter. Food and tobacco are ground into the dirty floor, already littered with rotting meat and soiled clothes. In the foreground a stripper gets ready for her act and, in preparation, provocatively adjusts her stockings. It would be hard for her to adjust them any other

way...

Tom's life appears only in dirty colours throughout. Browns and reds that imply Guinness and steak and kidney pie – painted in the style of bawdy humour for the Working Man and intended for the walls of Public Houses. Even the bleakest, 'greyest' places seem to portray flesh and stench, to be depicted in a way that is somehow evocative of gout.

There are opportunities for redemption later on, Sarah reappears, weeps and writes letters, but predictably it is all to no avail. Tom, a poor, poor boy, stupid and abroad, has developed such a taste for depravity that only destitution and madness can follow. He is taken first to the Fleet prison for unpaid debts. Then, when this drives him mad, to Bedlam and his story's wounded end.

Alice, for obvious reasons, did not immediately take to *The Rake's Progress*.

'It was the basis for an opera. Stravinsky wrote it,' said Camilla with firm gentleness. Camilla rather liked *The Rake's Progress*. Sometimes Camilla just liked what she liked as opposed to being sophisticated. Sometimes Camilla would e-mail you a picture of a cat dressed as a cow. It was charming in the way of the red room or that the Greek columns on one of the semis on the street where Alice grew up might be. She appreciated this but –

'That would have been in a different *style*,' she said. She did not want to be convinced. 'This man paints in mucky colours.'

They left the Hogarths and went to look at some Canalettos. *A View of St Mark's Square* and *The Rialto Bridge*. Hogarth had reputedly been a great patriot. Amongst other things, he had founded a society for British beef. He had probably never been to Italy. They looked at the Canalettos for a bit.

The weather was milder and Camilla was wearing a riding jacket. Alice had on her paisley scarf. Camilla was wearing her white leather gloves.

Alice's were black leather because her environment was less clean generally.

'Will you invite anyone from the gallery? Are they highbrow?' said Alice.

'Their style is highbrow,' said Camilla, 'but their essence is middle management. These days I expect nothing from art.'

'Really?' said Alice. 'These days it's the *only* thing I expect anything from.'

Secretly she felt relieved, as she was always relieved, when successful people failed to live up to expectation. It implied that there was no great hurry to do anything straight away. The fourth painting needed space to evolve – a beautiful highbrow tortoise who would ultimately win the race. Alice told Camilla about *Fuck Dance Lets Art*. Camilla said she'd like to go, but maybe not, as there was a private view on in Rivington Street – a political Belgian artist – that same night, and that someone else who was going owed her a gram of coke.

They drifted away from painting and middle management and into a bright yellow silk room full of upholstery and endless curtains. There was little else. Alice felt that it was the best room so far. After two seconds it sank in and then they moved on again. That was how they did museums – round and around in a daze of conversation, back and forth between well framed glimpses. Their words had context, complemented each scene, in the yellow room a silence, a while later a continuation.

'How's the exhibition coming along?' said Camilla, a few minutes later, and against a backdrop of high art.

'Chris wants it to be 'controversial *and* aggressive',' said Alice, and laughed and shook her head like it wasn't important.

They had walked and circled and were now back in front of *The Rake's Progress*. Camilla took off her gloves and touched the surface while the attendant wasn't looking. Earlier Alice had wanted to touch the lips of a marble bust. She removed her gloves also and accidentally dropped one on the floor. She bent down to pick it up, and then stood up again too quickly. A rush of blood to the head. She felt momentarily unsteady.

'Chris isn't a mystery. Chris is a void. I feel obliged to point that out,' said Camilla.

'Right.'

Alice wished she had bought grey gloves instead. Grey didn't show the dirt either and it was more edgy than black. An elegant non-colour that would have matched her funnel-necked coat, a noncommittal colour like filmic smog. The black pair had been bought on impulse.

'They have Neoclassical sculpture in the basement. Should we do that?' said Alice.

'I'm not bothered.'

'I'm not.'

They linked arms and continued their promenade of the upper floors. They moved back downstairs to the red room. It was a lovely room. Alice took both her gloves off and put them in her bag. Camilla did the same. They were women who understood the power of an image and alabaster lacked the tactile warmth of paint.

'This is my favourite room,' said Camilla, and moved her hair back from her face so as to create a perfect back to front cameo. Alice wondered if she had been here before without telling, been on her own and looked in the mirrors in the red room. For a long time. Sometimes they were still similar.

'I liked the yellow room more. It feels like you're inside the sun,' said Alice. 'But here you are the sun.' And Camilla's image orbited from mirror to mirror around the room.

Alice laughed and turned on her heel and her world laughed with her, four times and in unison. It was a beautifully composed cosmos where Sir John Soane linked to Mr Wallace to Hogarth to her dropped glove and a burning silk room of sun. Alice threw her gloves in the air and laughed.

Party

Camilla opened the door to her small gathering through a haze of pistachio Chanel. Yes. It was definitely Chanel. *And where you lead I cannot follow* thought Alice.

'Chanel?' said Alice, the possessor of two lipsticks, a reader of magazines, and smiled. They exchanged kisses. Chris handed over the usual bottle of mid-priced red wine and gave a nod. He was wearing a strange shirt, and he pulled at the collar with nervous irritation. They were mainly Alice's friends.

'That's a sweet dress. We've both gone frothy,' said Camilla, and tugged a ruffle with (well-practised) playful poise. Her intellect had a style to it. She said flip things, but knew they were flip but meant them all the same. That was the style. It allowed for pistachio where lesser mortals would have felt the sugar rot set in.

And Alice knew that tonight people would want to talk to her because she was that type of person. That people asked her to parties and liked to say they were acquainted because despite the grubby confines of Hackney Wick, or maybe even because of them, despite a certain dead feeling, she owned an intimidating knowingness. This in turn endorsed a certain confidence. It meant that when she named a concert or book she never doubted that it was the *right* one. That she automatically knotted her scarf in the *right* way or bought a new thing first. It wasn't something worked at, it was innate, and girls who didn't have it annoyed her, seemed somehow stupid, inferior women.

Camilla linked Alice's arm and drew her inside (the gentle crunch of compacted snow under foot), and they were faced by a formless, ostentatious glow of light wood beige, chrome fittings and clean. Prints of Russian Constructivist paintings were stuck up on the far wall because the party had a theme and suddenly she noticed Camilla's badge – Lenin's face in a red star, edged in gold with a hammer and sickle – was currently riding a muted, fabric, wave. Camilla noticed her notice:

'I think our generation's become terribly apathetic. We need to start taking sides again,' she said, with real concern as mock concern, and readjusted her left lapel politics. Camilla laughed hard with intent. Alice laughed too. It was so nice to have a friend who spoke the same language and wore a badge.

She let her arm drop and moved over towards the Smeg fridge. She felt her skirt, of the right cut and length and pattern, swish against her rather good legs. She nearly, but didn't, pout. Other girls pouted, not her, and she felt that it implied too much neediness. Instead she twisted a stray piece of hair around her finger, and thought about the way her skirt moved when she did. Over the far end of the room she could see Armond racking out lines and raised her glass a fraction. He raised his glass back, in on the permanent joke, and passed a rolled up fifty to a man in a remarkable tie. What the joke was no one knew for sure, but they had decided to be in on it and in on it together. Later she would watch him offer up another line, then another, insisting, like a satanic Scout-master, that they all held hands with a long-dead demon and joined him in his heart-pounding avalanche game. He wouldn't let you say no, and no one ever really tried.

The man in the remarkable tie spat in Armond's face and diseased hyena shrieks flew out and around the room. Armond then pinned him to the sofa and spat repeatedly into his eye. There were more shrieks, more spitting and some slapping, until they tired themselves out and reeled back again, a pair of winding-down mechanical toys, checked their clothes, their hair, and then racked out another line.

The breeze from an opened door made Alice's skirt flutter-up, ever so slightly over her thighs, and she could see Chris watching out the corner of his eye. Alice let her eyelids close in a second's rapt superiority. Her new shoes were an elegant design of pink punched leather, kitten-heeled, and ending in a long narrow point. *Women don't live for love,* thought Alice, invincible, assured, *but for these moments of greatness.* She searched vaguely for a corkscrew, which she couldn't find, and then sat down beside him. Pink and white all over. Shiny hair, hazel eyes – *Oh Alice your taste is so exquisite* – satin ribbon, costume jewellery pearls, it didn't matter who noticed or who said it just so long as it was known and said, and exhilaration as everything rubbed off on everything.

There was a girl styled a bit like Nico, who put a Velvet Underground record on. She had a thick blonde fringe and kohl-rimmed eyes. *Perhaps she is too* exactly *like Nico* thought Alice. She was one of Camilla's sort of friends from the gallery. She looked like she used to go to Trash.

'Did you used to go to Trash?' said Alice, but the music was too loud to be heard.

These days the old Trash lot went to Nag Nag Nag or to Cashpoint, which was on a boat once a week. It was an older crowd with less indie music and more transsexuals. A similar amount of war paint. In another years time they would go to Electro Go-Go... But this girl, this other girl, she could tell was not adaptable, would have been the same then as now, whereas

Alice Grisham, in her wonderful dress and her wonderful shoes, well, Alice Grisham was always one step ahead...

All the Grade A-Gays were out in force and, consequently, the electroclash contingent. A nest of designer-clad vipers with Armond shining sombre in their midst. Fendi shoes in swastika red. The terrifying side parting. He racked out more lines. A little line for everyone to lift them higher up together and be happy on *his* terms and share in *the* joke. The Nag Nag Nag crowd morphed into the British/Russian Art crowd, and became an over spilling crowd of the beautiful people rising higher and higher and higher. Higher! Higher! Higher! Oh! The joy of sophisticated vice! Armond made neat little lines of powder on a marble coaster and offered them to the Hoxton girls opposite.

Lara took the coaster first for herself and then offered it to Lucy. They were talking non-stop, chain smoking Marlboro lights, and drinking White Russians. Lara was wearing a slash necked asymmetric top in fuicha by Vivienne Westwood Anglomania. Again the cleavage. Lucy wore the same, with the exception of her top being from House Of Jazz and one shoulder length earring in fluorescent lime Perspex. The colours clashed and jarred like warring parrots. Lara was re-telling Lucy about the time she had worked with Rosin Murphy. Lucy wasn't listening:

'Where's John? I like John,' said Lucy, Lara's friend, a party friend of Alice and Camilla's.

Alice explained that John was in Glasgow being decent and visiting his sister. Lucy looked disappointed for a second and then it was forgotten. She did another line. Lara looked bored. She changed the subject and said the mullet was completely over.

'Even Tommy Guns says no more mullets,' said Lara.

It was indisputable. A time had passed. Lara had had a mullet until recently, and an ironic Kiss jacket. Now she had a heavy fringe and black eyeliner in an up-dated rock look. Alice didn't care for irony, a stance that was becoming fashionable, but she liked Lara's fringe, which was similar to her own, and to Lucy's, and to Camilla's. Lara was attractive in an intense way that meant the men who didn't fancy her sometimes said she was a dog.

Lara resumed telling them about Rosin Murphy while no one listened. A haggard, unknown man crept up on her -

'Ay, Cleopatra,' he said, and poked Lucy in the ribs. He didn't look involved in either art or gayness and he was offensive without trying. Alice searched for a context and concluded that he must be Armond's dealer. *Crass*, thought Alice with her increasingly long learned vowels. She felt in danger of reaching a place where his red skin existed only as an interesting medical case study. *Heyhs craahs*, thought Alice, teetering on the chasm's edge, and it felt positively cut glass.

'Ay, Cleopatra', he said it again and touched Lucy's hair. 'I like yer 'air.'

Lucy looked appalled while the stranger began to laugh. Alice looked at the floor and took in his scuffed heels. She was a lower-middleclass provincial – the worse kind of snob. *I'm experimenting with tolerance*, it was accompanied by a guilty inward laughter, he was too removed – unaesthetic and unfamiliar – and a shard of glass lodged itself in her heart.

The stranger left them. The conversation continued.

Lara was excited about her new job for Sleazenation, and her new boyfriend, who Alice had met, who was a typographer for Dazed. Lucy was excited about the jewellery that she made that was now being sold in Brown's Focus. Lara was still concerned about the death of the mullet. Surely if Tommy Guns, creator of the modern mullet, said no more mullets, then that meant Tommy Guns was also out. Lara had tried a new hairdresser's off Brick Lane, but the standard just wasn't as good. They had used the old fashioned metal straighteners instead of the new ceramic ones and you'd never get that at Tommy Guns, but then they were supposed to be over. Had Alice tried the new ceramic straighteners? Lara could get them for her at a discount price.

She had a connection. She was hair aware. Did Alice straighten her hair because it already looked quite straight naturally?

Lucy revealed that she didn't straighten her hair because her hair was the opposite of Lara's. It was fine and fly-away. She was considering a perm, partly for volume. So much time had passed that perms might be avant-garde again by now, but she wasn't entirely sure. Chris' hair looked like it might be avant-garde, was it? For the time being she was sticking with her big fringe rock look, which was a modern classic.

Alice did a little line to keep up. It kicked in and she had a lot to say about ceramic straighteners. Her knee touched Chris's. Her awkward, beautiful-kneed, shadow.

Her knee touched Chris.

After a while talk faltered and Lucy went over to the record player. She took the Velvet Underground off and put the Moldy Peaches on. She turned the volume up. Lara began dancing with two of the A-Gays one of whom was wearing a large fur hat. He had a homemade t-shirt saying 'From Russia With Love,' which was contemporary. He drew a red star on Lara's cheek in lipstick and eyeliner because Lara had forgotten that there was a theme but still wanted to join in. Robotic neon dance moves flashed from the far corner and the record jumped. Over the noise Camilla and Armond could be heard discussing the advantages of Botox.

'Well it's something to do,' he was saying. 'And it shows that you're *maintained*. I find it hard to look at people who don't *maintain* themselves. It's so much more insulting than just being ugly.'

There followed a short lull in conversation, during which Armond cut two more fat lines for Camilla and himself. They were getting on so well. And Camilla was genuinely interested in Botox. She might have it in a few years, but then by that time another method of non-intrusive surgery might be fashionable or, depending on how she looked, she might want to put the money towards a modern classic like a Barcelona chair.

The music continued. Lucy joined in the dancing. Crispin, Camilla's boyfriend, or partner as she had taken to calling him since the move into commercial art, began handing out more White Russians. He was wearing a Miu Miu twin set for men in smooth knit grey, and a tie at a deliberately casual angle. He went to offer Alice a drink and tripped. Milk spilled out onto the beech work surface and was instantly cleaned away. He repositioned his tie and folded the dishcloth back into a neat square. Alice complemented him on the party. Such a nice flat, such nice people, and everyone looking so great, and the cocktails, well, just so Eastern Bloc chic.

'Thanks,' said Crispin, 'we meant to do food but couldn't think of anything Russian. I made some cous cous earlier, but it's still in the fridge. We decided it was a Nineties' carbohydrate.'

Alice took her drink and sat down again. While she'd been away a girl had begun talking to Chris. It was the same girl who had put The Velvet Underground on earlier. Up close her blonde fringe was badly cut. Alice knew her type – rich kids that travelled extensively in their gap years, all conceited ignorance and indifference to money – and then the usual guilt for the usual meanness. She met a lot of girls like this. They studied Art History and got jobs in galleries. They studied English Literature and got jobs in publishing. Chris' posture relaxed slightly. He was comfortable now, as the familiarity of superior irritation combined with the possibility of easy sex. He sat with his legs planted firmly apart leaning in towards the girl, and his knee touched Alice's for the second time. He began to wax lyrical:

'What I plan on doing is going into promotions. It's where the money is. Work hard for a year or so to gain the experience. Then buy a property – maybe here, maybe New York – probably here. Stay near my family. I value my family – '

Chris smoothed back the Mafioso hair and lengthened his stride. It was the first time he had spoken all evening. The gallery had not worked out, and so he searched for something else to stamp it on. He ran his hand through his hair in typically high-powered breakdown mode as though art had never really mattered, was just another line aimed at getting girls and looking cool, and as though 'promotions', whatever that meant, whatever the terrible, useless thing that didn't need promoting was, could just as easily take it's place. Alice smiled thinly at Chris and Nico. She rearranged her imitation pearls. She wondered what Chris would do next.

Next, Chris produced his new camera. Alice suspected that he'd brought it along to try and take pictures of girls for later, because he did things like that sometimes – things like deliberately searching out the cheapest porno mags where the girls looked really real, or wanking under the duvet at Wimbledon's Women's Doubles – but thought that no one cottoned on.

'It's the best model on the market,' Chris said, and stroked the casing with a masturbator's eye.

Alice did another line, while still very high from the one before, and watched them both, unblinking and better dressed. She watched Nico, in particular, who seemed impressed. Her shy fingers reached out towards the camera that lay cradled in Chris' still Nietzsche-scarred hands. Chris smirked. Nico smiled. A small blizzard covered the coffee table, and the tragicomedy chipped at Alice's glass heart. She could hear Lucy shouting out if anyone had brought any more pills, and Lara telling her she was being annoying. In the background Armond was pushing a bottle up another A-Gays arse while they both cackled vacuously.

The other night Alice had dreamt about Chris and her. They had been walking through a field in the snow. Chris had lain down and folded his arms across his chest and let the snow begin to cover him. It was incredibly cold. Alice had known that if he stayed like that in the snow he would die. She had tried to tell him this. To pull him up and out of the snow. To brush the flakes out of his eyes and pull him up, but he wouldn't listen. Eventually she'd had to leave him – they couldn't both die – and run off alone through the snow, cold and sick. When she had woken up she'd been crying. Weak silent tears and the shame of unreciprocated emotion.

'Ay, ay!' the Mancunian was back, and poked her now, 'you look like, dead, dead – ' he wavered for a second, a rabbit caught in the headlights of a room full of dark fringed girls, searching for recognition, or a context even – 'like intellectual!'

'Now that's just offensive.' But it was delivered softly, because even his red fingers seemed ravaged by excess, and because to look him in the eye unflinching was to stare down fear. Alice looked away. She looked out and away and into the beige.

From a distance she was able to get a proper look at Chris' collar. The two long narrow points, higher up and closer together on his neck than a usual shirt collar, were somehow uncanny. She thought that he would surely have had to alter an existing shirt to make it look that way. You couldn't possibly buy a shirt with weirdo detailing like that. Not in London. But why do such a thing? Why – and then, and then – he was copying *Goodfellas*! That's what it was. That's where she had seen that look before. He was trying for a Scorsese-look collar!

Chris was the only person that Alice liked but did not understand. At times she feared that this was the only attraction. At times she felt painfully helpless.

More people arrived. Alice sort of knew some of them. Some of the men Lara hung out with, though not Geoff, Lara's new boyfriend, and a girl called Laura from the magazine. Laura sat down next to Lara and began discussing the new ceramic straighteners, which she was worried might be bad for your hair. Alice joined in and got them all another drink. Lara found an E in her pocket and crushed it up with some coke. Laura did a little line while

Lucy jumped up and started dancing with Lara's boyfriend and his friends. Laura said that if they all put in she could get some more coke.

Lucy began wriggling up to all the men in a seductive style. She flicked her hair and bit her bottom lip. She wriggled particularly close to Lara's boyfriend. She pressed up against all of them in turn, laughing and grinding and tossing her head back. Pouting. She turned round and rubbed herself up against Lara's boyfriend like a girl in a hip-hop video, shaking her loving, denim sprayed arse.

Alice rearranged her imitation pearls for the second time and looked at Lucy. *Silly cow*, she thought, *you're rich not black.* Then she looked at Lara and raised an eyebrow. Lara looked at Lucy and scowled. Lucy didn't notice. Then Lara turned back to Alice, Laura and the straightners. They were ok on your hair, provided you had a day off now and again and used a deep conditioning treatment occasionally. Alice went to get more drinks. Lucy wriggled up to Chris. A girl called Lilly arrived and started making a spliff.

Crispin was making more White Russians, and Alice went over to congratulate him on his choice of glasses. They discussed the glasses. Armond joined them and gave his opinion on the glasses which was the same as Alice's – the *right* one. Crispin was really fucked. He refused another line of coke. Armond suggested he do another line again. Several times. Ceaselessly. Eventually Crispin gave in and did another line.

'I'm generous to a fault,' said Armond, and his eyes shone with distorted sincerity.

'What do you think about Martini glasses? Are they kitsch or sophisticated or both?' said Alice, who discussed different things with different people, and currently wanted to discuss glasses. A contemplative silence followed.

'I think they're alright so long as you only serve Martini in them,' Armond said finally. 'Other drinks might look naff.'

'Camilla is thinking of investing in some Martini glasses but tumblers are more versatile,' said Crispin. He rearranged his tie, and stood there in a clean and well-pressed manner. He picked up an unused tumbler and handed it to Alice for her and Armond's more detailed inspection. They were exquisite glasses. They looked at the glasses in silence.

'Chris is going into Promotion' said Alice, in order to fill it.

Armond smiled sideways. He was already racking out the next gram with his gold card. There had never been a night out without Armond taking copious amounts of coke. Perhaps he was an addict and empty cobwebs inside. Perhaps he just liked a good time. *Maybe he will have another heart attack*, thought Alice in an absent way, while they all continued to discuss the tumblers. They were a heavy, minimal crystal, practically a necessity.

Chris joined them.

'I hear you're venturing into the world of promotions?' said Armond, and Chris appeared momentarily unnerved. 'I can see it now, a rough diamond like yourself climbing to the top through sheer grit. Smart suit, penthouse flat, blowjobs off high-class prostitutes in the back of your sports car. I've got a hard-on just thinking about it.'

Alice pictured a Lamborghini Countach – the top car in Top Trumps – and filled it with whores. And if Alice could see it, then they all could see it. It was all highly probable and typically uneasy. Was it already that point in the evening? Thrashing, tail-biting eels in a bucket? The platinum egotist relented and racked out another line for Chris. Alice anxiously picked up the tumbler to show him and soften things, she felt guilty for telling, but –

'Actually, I went to see a prostitute the other week,' said Chris. He was properly gone. His appeared to be leering, his eyes half-shut and clouded by jism, though perhaps he was just badly lit. 'I thought I'd try anything once but it's weird. Seventy quid for a bird that looks like your mother to suck your cock and then she finishes and then it's like "Fuck off mother." I wouldn't go again.'

This was the room in which psychoanalysis took place.

Chris was oblivious. He didn't understand which bit was the shocking bit or why. He did the next line, stepped out in front of the oncoming traffic, and continued.

'I mean some guys don't get it that often, not good looking like what I am, so it's different. But I was on the football team at school and everything. I always got pussy. I don't need it so bad.'

There was a stunned silence from the sublimated elite. They were used to the style of debauchery. To the squeals and grimaces and extravagant disordered giggles. But this was different. This was Klaus Kinski playing Hemingway while the crowd bayed for blood. And it was appalling. Camilla began to laugh. As did Armond. As did Crispin. It was the only sane response. Chris looked confused, then shrugged. He dabbed at powder traces with a wet finger and rubbed it on his gums.

He was the only person Alice liked but did not understand. She looked out, away, tainted by a painful, womanly tenderness, and still she existed.

Nico was dancing with two of her male equivalents, Lucy, Lara and the secondary A-gays. They were playing Peaches now, and other German electro. One of the men kept trying to catch her eye. He was quite good looking with dark curls and cords. Last year she might have fancied him. She gave him a smile, and a song later he reached an arm out to circle her waist. Alice wriggled free, stepped neatly over to the other side of the group and looked away. Only a minor awkwardness, a second later it was forgotten.

And a second later she regretted it being forgotten. What was she playing at? She tried to win him back and catch his eye, but now he was catching the eye of Nico, the gallery girl, who seemed keen. *Slag*, thought Alice without really thinking. Camilla and Crispin came over and joined in the dancing. Someone had put on Chicks on Speed and everyone was off their heads and going for it.

'Apparently Krakow is the new East Berlin,' said Alice, and they all agreed.

Soon everyone was dancing. The good-looking man and the gallery girl had moved over to the sofa and started snogging, him frantically pushing one hand up under her skirt, into her pants, her self-conscious, but going with it. Alice laughed and looked at Chris who shrugged his shoulders and smiled. They were all dancing. They all thought they were good dancers.

'Is it true that Alison Goldfrapp has a stylist?' said Camilla. Lara nodded. Unfortunately it was.

Mark, she had discovered that that was Armond's dealer's name, was dancing. He pushed his way into the middle of the circle and began jerking his arms about. He was very red and a lot older than the rest of them. He looked out of breath. Someone said he used to manage a band that had once been famous. He was still involved in music and the drugs were just a sideline. He was managing a new band that would be big very soon. He was looking at Camilla, who had ceramically straightened dark hair with a fringe.

'Ay! Cleopatra! Cleopatra! What yous doing?'

'What?' Camilla paused mid step. A White Russian half way towards her lips as every dark haired girl merged into one.

'Ow whass the matter with all yous crazy artists? Are yous gonna sacrifice us fer bein' from Manchastar or something?'

Someone turned the volume up. The gallery girl and the good-looking boy sneaked off into the toilet together. Someone Else dropped a White Russian and a vodka/milk mixture sloshed across the floor. The man in the remarkable tie had turned all the heating up and poured poppers over the radiators. He took all his clothes off, bar the tie, and continued dancing. Lucy began dancing with him in her underwear and heels. She kept laughing and falling over. She kept rubbing her tits through her see-through bra shouting 'Let's make a movie. C'mon lets make a moooooooooooooooovie!' While no one paid her much attention. Sometimes she fell over onto Lara's new boyfriend and had to steady herself through a hand placed too far up on his thigh. 'I wanna make a movie so let's star in it together,' screeched tunelessly out while her nails dug firmly into his leg. Lara looked on glassy-eyed, and Laura asked her some more questions about hairdressers. Lara gave an impressively detailed response.

Armond was dancing with Camilla. He lifted her high above his head, then slipped in the milk and fell over, tumbling them both on top of Alice. Camilla's skirt was hitched up over her legs. She wasn't wearing any knickers. Armond pulled her skirt fully up over her head and lace and milk and an axe wound exposed. Lucy threw herself on top of the heap to join in. She stuck out her leg and tripped Lara's new boyfriend up so that he fell down heavily on top of her.

Alice felt leaden. Outside it was the cold grey light of early dawn, and the music switched to Joy Division.

Hackney Wick IV

The stars conjoined to lend the journey home unnecessary romance. It wasn't windy, but still enough of a chill for Chris to place his jacket around her shoulders. Close up of his arm remaining a second too long. Cut to shot of a lingering look. A full moon, a clear sky, a man, a woman, art and pessimism – Alice's life would always be filmed in black and white.

The coke was wearing off, and they were nearly home.

'Well that was glamorous,' Chris was saying, with heavy sarcasm, 'Empty? Yes. Repulsive? Yes. But glamorous. Aren't you glamorous Alice? Alice, aren't you and all your cool friends cool?'

He pulled her arm tightly all the while, so as to force her towards him and ensure she looked and listened. He carried on ranting, as if he hadn't accepted the drugs, or tried to fuck the gallery girl. As if she'd bought greedily into it while he held back, clear-eyed and apart. He gripped her too tightly and it hurt.

Alice shrugged him off. Chris tried again to pull her back, more gently this time, but she was upset. She thrust the jacket back at him and pushed past. As she did so, a very expensive frill caught on a railing and tore. It was too much. She was immersed in an ungovernable rage, span on her heel and hissed-

'You're a boring bastard, a self-centred, boring bastard, who says the same thick things over and over again and ought to be bored of being alive!'

It didn't quite make sense but it kind of made the point. Her fists were clenched tight against her sides as she marched on ahead. It wasn't as if he'd had to come. The way he always had to have the last word – it was pitiable. He shouldn't have come and she wouldn't have cared. She turned round again –

'You're really fucking boring!' and continued to walk on as fast as she could. She was determined not to cry and looked upwards just in case. Her nails dug in against the palms of her hands and she thought how she must get home straight away. That it was imperative she be allowed to take off her horrible dress as soon as possible, and shut the door, and then cry and cross her fingers 'til the morning, because they'd been to a great party, a really great party, and she'd honestly never been to a better one... And then, just as she turned into their street but before she reached the door, came Chris from behind her –

'Alice wait, I'm sorry, I know they're your mates.' He was strangely pleading in a way she hadn't heard before, 'I think I'm just a bit paranoid from the coke. I know sometimes I say stupid things, but it's only for something to say, and anyway, that party *was* shit. It just made me feel lonely and old. *You know what I mean.*'

The conviction was overwhelming. He honestly believed these emotions unique to him. He glanced fleetingly at the CCTV camera by the lift, then back at her with a hounded look. She always knew he was epic. And literature confirmed it. It added to the moonlight. *The serious moonlight.* She was so glad they weren't on Bowie Art. There was a long and loaded pause and then –

'You looked very pretty tonight.'

He blurted it out quickly, awkward and unintended by the industrial lift shaft. It came out so awkward she thought it must be at least a little meant – and thought then of that day on the beach when he wasn't happy. She saw him dead in the snow and refusing to be saved. There was an ache that belonged in a space beyond education.

'You like a lot of girls,' she said because she had to, as a last chance plea for reassurance and a get-out clause. And because they were both young and read the same books, and saw the same films. And because he had had bad skin when he was younger, and had scars on his hands from putting his hand through a window, and often got it really, stupidly, wrong.

'No, I fuck a lot of girls. I like hardly any of them. But I like you Alice. I – I care about you. I – I – You know what I'm trying to say!'

And Alice thought: *he is so beautiful; he is so incredibly beautiful that it leaves me faint and hideous.* Because he always told the truth. He always meant the things he said and wasn't dead inside.

He has lovely eyes, thought Alice. *His hair is just a phase, but when he smiles it's really quite nice.* A little drunk still, a little high still, but still a little truth seeped in.

Outside now, heavy rain.

She shivered. The rain beat down against the glass. The camera would have filmed backs of heads and hands. Cut between them haphazardly and played each moment a moment too long. It was at a point where now inevitable. A New Wave love affair.

They are back inside the warehouse now and kissing. Their mouths are stale and alcoholic.

And *Bang! He shot me down.*

Alice loved Nancy Sinatra.

And *Bang! I hit the ground.*

She was considerably less keen on the version by Cher.

Alice closes her eyes and pictures earth fall softly onto her face. Fine sand-like grains that cover her eyes and nose and mouth. Gently, wilfully falling.

And then it is over.

They both express a degree of shyness. Chris does up his belt and looks away, embarrassed. Alice picks at a now missing button.

'I messed up the interview for Rome,' she says. 'I think it was when I began to talk about the frequent disappointment of *actual* experience, and consequently the transcendence of art – painting in particular – that it really fell apart.' Her laughter is of the nervous kind which abrupt silence always follows. Chris mentions an article in *Artforum* that she might like to read. It is apparent that communal living has taken on a new horror, and each departs, alone, to their separate beds.

A terrible dangerous terrible thing had happened. He slept while she didn't, and a friendship crumbled into insignificance. A time had passed.

Sigh, reader. *Sigh.*

Part 4

Hackney Wick V

Predictably, things in the Warehouse degenerated. Chris brought another girl home within a week. She had a fat, glossed mouth, and the overtly sexual mannerisms of the borderline attractive. Together they produced a budget and affected type of noise, while on the other side of the plasterboard wall Alice felt herself go limp from idiocy.

And then, of course, there were other things. Like the credit card bills which had mounted up, or the rent that was due. There was the council tax, the bank loan, the student loan and the debt collector. They were the indebted generation. That's what they had claimed, as gleefully another bottle was opened, another cigarette lit. Terrorism was a legitimate threat these days. The future categorically uncertain. *So let's keep dancing. Let's roll out the booze and have a good time.* The radio played Peggy Lee and the tap still dripped.

Alice walked over to the kitchen area and in doing so stubbed her toe.

She picked up the offensive object, now out of its videocassette casing, and nearly placed it in the bin. Okay, so they had sold their souls for the glamour of perpetual nihilism, wallowed in their stunted childhoods, and given it all for the moment in their decrepit man made hovel – but what happened when the moment passed? And what had happened to the fourth painting? To the music? To the soul singer singing, her voice a step past language – nearly breaking – as she reached the highest point and sang of love and loss?

The spring wind blew cold around Hackney Wick, the rain fell in sheets – lately it was always raining – and the starter homes were nearly finished. She recalled how only a few days ago John claimed to have overheard a girl in explicitly fashionable legwarmers commenting that the area was, 'The New Hoxton'. Rumour had it a gastro-pub was about to be opened their end of Victoria Park. In short, people who could afford to live in better places were coming here on purpose, complete with their organic shopping and urge to gentrify. Their days of Wild West living would soon be over, only an image, a false and sepia tinted memory of the days before they were bored. As an unwatched pornographic film slipped from a weak white hand, Alice Grisham, scared of change, fearful of rotting, looked out of the window and sighed into a non-reflective surface.

'Bring out your dead,' said Alice to the Ikea shelving unit, but couldn't be bothered to cry. The living area was deserted, a desolate landscape of non-washed dreams. The phone trilled out over the radio, over the filth of long ago parties, and was ignored. Outside the rain continued sympathetically, nature harmonious and picturesque. Well at least there would always be beauty – sometimes the philosophy was enough.

She began to clear the table, boil the kettle, and scrape ashy, eggy plates. She removed a tea stained gas bill from underneath the major debris. She stacked the magazines in a pile under the shelving unit, made a half-hearted attempt at a sticky patch and brewed coffee in John's Heals' cafetiére. A splash of coffee landed on her baby pink baby doll pyjamas. She was still in her pyjamas and not yet showered. Limp strands of hair fell on pallid cheeks. An unerupted pimple throbbed menacingly beneath the skin.

Alice dabbed the splash with the sponge and made sure it was properly gone, then found some spot cream and applied it as a preventative measure. Two of her books, she noticed, expensive exhibition catalogues, were in John's section of the bookshelf. There was a torn page in one of the introductions. She put it back in her section.

Other possible futures were considered as she began to put cds, some of which were scratched, in an old shoebox. She wanted to be particular with her packing and leave no untidiness, and therefore no blame. To pack it neatly in boxes. Labelled even. She noticed that one of her cds had been scratched. She put it in the shoe-box. She would pay the rent until the end of the month and make sure they found someone reasonable to live in her place. She thought briefly that they would be best off with another man, or a sensible, older girl with a boyfriend – but supposed that as ultimately this was now beyond her control it warranted little other thought. Hackney Wick was already no more than a quaint and failed manifesto, one of *passive immobility and slumber,* done and dusted and buried and dead.

Alice crawled underneath the coffee table. It was a tight fit, and as she wriggled sharp corners poked at her exposed knees and thighs. She began to ease the top off its steel frame until eventually the heavy sheet of glass, now free of all supports, lay flat and crushingly over her. Alice shut her eyes. The pins and needles crept slowly, hinting at the oncoming numbness, which, like love, a torn page or a scratched disc, would soon become just another test of what one was able to endure.

Credits

Mary-Marie knocked on Alice's door. She was super keen to be Alice's super best friend. This alone was off putting.

'Wow! Look at you! You look like me!' said Mary-Marie with all of a wiggle and public school gush. She smiled, as though this wasn't a strange, or openly inflated, thing to say, and simultaneously attempted an arm squeeze.

A guttural cough constituted Alice's response. She wondered how on earth Marie-Marie, silly little thing that she was, could ever have thought such a silly little thing up. Then she remembered that she didn't want to be a snob, that one should help those less fortunate than oneself, that people needed people and here was one she had to live with. She tried to smile back by way of compensation, and then opened the door in a further lame try at kindness.

Alice Grisham, our recently re-located snip-snap of a plaything, was wearing a brand new turquoise waffle knit jumper by Marc Jacobs, chocolate brown silk stockings, a brown tweed skirt with a highly sharp, even avant-garde, ruche and vintage brown, gold and turquoise sling backs with an equally revolutionary heel. Chloe Sevingy had been wearing something similar in last month's American Vogue. And, as she flitted, snip-snap and kingfisher bright, from window gazing delight, to door opening duty, she considered this likeness to a well-known off-beat icon, and decided not only that this was the principal issue at stake, but also the one her new acquaintance was, sadly, least likely to understand.

Mary-Marie, who was wearing a turquoise pashmina in, admittedly, the same shade as the waffle knit, positioned herself so as to try for a second squeeze while Alice darted quickly away.

'Mary-Marie,' she half-wanted but couldn't quite be bothered to say, 'Mary-Marie of suburban tastes and morals, are you a little obsessed by me, the owner of a superior wardrobe and flattened vowels of a provincial Northerner?'

But all things pass, and there was a door here, which could be shut when knocked upon, and had been shut often, and with a sense of great relief. Mary-Marie wasn't someone she would ever have chosen for herself, but then neither was she inescapable. And this counted, was considerable, and today was all that mattered. And all things pass, and Alice was a heavy stone, not something flimsy to be blown by the wind.

'No, I mean really, like really, wow! You've finished your beautiful painting! Wow!'

And so there it was. Not necessarily *the* fourth painting, not necessarily beautiful, but *a* forth painting. Complete and of the world.

Let us pause for a moment, away from recent events and prying, motivated eyes, to contemplate what this may actually *mean*. Alice Grisham, a predominantly intelligent young woman, concerned by the legitimate threat of terrorism, in thrall to material goods, and living in fear of the camera phone, has completed a work of art. She has done so outside of an educational institution, and with no expectation of wealth or notoriety. Reader, ambition is *limiting* – double wow.

The dimensions of this work are therefore immaterial. Likewise Alice's choice of colours, textures, representations and abstractions. What do they matter when pressed up close against the mind-blowing notion of completion? Indeed, why not lean in and press yourself closer to me? Why not lean in until you feel my breath on your face and see my pupils dilate with longing? Come closer, wrap your arms around me, place your ear against my heart and listen to its painful beat:

The fourth painting is less than exceptional.

Now that's not to say it's bad. It might even be better than the previous three that were fine. Which were fine, fine art from a fine, fine artist, and sold like the proverbial hot cakes. It's better than a lot of the stuff on the (whisper it) market, the pseudo-intellectual crap of someone like, well we might as well say Mary-Marie, but we could say Nicki and Sam, Chris, Armond, even John, would and do produce. It's not bad, but it's not great either. It somehow fails to live up to the manifesto, to the talent for existence we would like to attribute to Alice, with her pretty clothes, her proficient refinements, her accomplished performance in the *artiste* role... There's nothing embarrassing about the fourth painting, it's very nice, but nice isn't convulsive – isn't beautiful. And it just, well, it *lacks*...

'Where will you hang it!? Who will you show it to!!?' An orgasm of exclamation marks. Mary-Marie beamed approval at all she did not understand but suspected might be relevant. 'I painted like that a couple of years ago!'

'Mary-Marie,' Alice wanted but wasn't quite cruel enough to say, 'I refuse to be anything less than indifferent to you and all like you because you are tame.'

'Probably behind the wardrobe,' she said instead, and was rewarded with an expression of demented hurt. 'I'd like to be on my own now.'

It came out slowly and clearly with the forced sweetness of an immense irritation. Lately Alice felt as though she had discovered how to be hard. Discovered how to compress the panic until it turned into stony composure, and she fought this rising nausea now, until her stomach became lined with steel and she tasted metal – blood and tinfoil – in the back of her throat. She swallowed hard – *let the waves crash* she would remain heavy and immovable – and made a move towards the door.

'I understand!' said Mary-Marie. She pressed Alice's hand for a little too long, and furrowed her brow in an expression she had witnessed in other people as concern. Alice continued to lead Mary-Marie gently towards the exit and then carefully manoeuvred her out of it. She shut the door quickly. Bolted it. Shut her eyes and refused to feel responsible. The soft earth fell gently down upon her. It was fine, almost sand-like, it covered her eyes, her nose, her mouth, drawing her deeper and deeper under. *Life is turning me into something indestructible*, she thought. *A black hole or... or... a deity!*

Alice's new room was a large and pleasant one of the kind imagined when these words are said. High, white, sanitised walls, wooden floorboards and a bay window overlooking the Highbury end of Clissold Park. She had furnished it, through money from her job, with only a few things but all of which were good quality and moderately expensive. There was a dark wood chest of drawers/dressing table that housed winter jumpers, underwear, stockings and tights. On top of this, a display of make-up and perfume (a gift from Camilla) at neat angles to each other, some ceramic straightening irons (at discount from Lara), and a mirror small and kindly enough not to let you look too close. The bed linen was matching and from Habitat – white broderie anglaise. And then there was a brown reed blind and slightly fey lamp that had belonged to one of Alice's various Great-Aunts. All books and records were arranged neatly and in alphabetical order. Shoes were kept inside their boxes with photographs of the shoes within the box taped to the side. Remaining clothes were on a rail behind a dark wood beaded curtain next to which was a poster, bought from the ICA bookshop, which boldly stated *Fuck Dance Lets Art*. She was still unsure as to whether she had always craved this order, or whether it simply acted as an Alka Seltzer after the prolonged night out which had been open-plan warehouse living in Hackney Wick. At any rate the result was soothing. The room smelt of bleach. There was a door that could be shut.

By the window was a glass vase of flowers and ferns. Alice went and knelt beside it. The light cut through her and the vase in a bright clear oblong, hit on smooth hair and clean-living skin. Her cheeks were a juvenile flush now, and a little of the old glamour seeped away. Framed against the interior and exterior, the park and the ferns, caught in a sharp bright shaft of light, a pink and white hand rearranges a fern. She sat by the window for a long time, pleased with the image. She stroked the ends of her hair and the tips of the ferns and looked out of the window. Someone had said there were deer in the park, but you couldn't see any from here. Alice felt a bit sad, but mainly calm. Everyone she knew was sad anyway, so it didn't really matter. She hummed a little and tapped her foot. Nothing ever really changes.

'Hiya!' There was a knock at the door. Alice unbolted the door, and then opened it a tiny crack. Mary-Marie wheedled through the crack, rubbed Alice's back in an overly affectionate way and sat down by the window. She had been shut out only a few minutes ago. Now here she was again, sat too close and smiling dumbly.

'I've got something to show you!'

They were sat too close. Alice shifted a little further to the left. 'Yes?'

She could already taste the iron in the back of her throat, a steel pincer reaching up within her and then retracting. She touched the ends of hair, the fern tips, soft, soft, soft – but something immovable.

'Have you heard of her?' said Mary-Marie, and held out a book by Susan Sontag.

'Yes.' said Alice, who had particularly like her essay, *On Style*, who had described herself as an avid reader on a Waterstones' application form, and felt resentful that the truth had proved to be an unadvantageous cliche.

'She's a famous art theorist.'

'Yes. I've heard of her.'

'She's a fiercely intelligent woman. You'd like her. I'm going to lend her to you.'

The book was further outstretched, and in a way that made it impossible to refuse. There was an uncomfortable acceptance on Alice's part, and an inward acknowledgement of unfair debt. She already had Camilla's Sade. Camilla had her Rimbaud. It was an already complete exchange that left no room for another book lending friend.

'She's a feminist!' added Marie-Marie brightly, as one Netball captain to another, 'like us!' And again pressed Alice's hand.

'No' said Alice. 'What you have to understand is that I'm too shallow and uptight to be that kind of fashion. I like buying things, clothes and books mainly, and then looking at them. That's all. I have no wish to progress beyond it.'

'What?' said Mary-Marie.

'I don't want to be a fesbian.'

'Fe*minist,* silly!'

Mary-Marie began to rearrange the ferns. Alice rearranged them back. Mary-Marie took the lid off a box of shoes and held one shoe up against her different sized foot. Alice took the shoe back, put it back in the box and put the lid back on. Other, similar things, in keeping with this theme, happened until eventually Mary-Marie was shifted back into the hall and the door firmly shut for a second time. Then she bolted it. And put a chair underneath the handle. It was an unnecessary gesture only in a fixed sense.

Alice looked back at the book. She turned it over in her small hands. On the back was a black and white photograph of the author and a publisher's blurb referring to the writer's strength and fierce intelligence. A small snort of laughter escaped. *How could a person be so entirely subscribed?* thought Alice. *How could someone begin already sure of their own conclusion?* She had never had any conclusions herself, other than that disaster was often inevitable but sometimes photogenic. An internet personality quiz had once termed her an existential thinker. She stroked the ends of her hair, and looked out of the window reassured. She shut her eyes and, for a moment, lightness.

And an all consuming freshness in the view of the park and the ferns in a glare of green together. A newness, a beginningness where all was not lost. The potential for freedom lies in the closing of an eyelid and as her fingertips touched green the purity of a languid faint lifted Alice high above the white. And there was no desire except for the moment itself, and no memory, only an emptiness soaring upwards, high above the canopy and yet not too close to the sun –

A sharp and sudden knocking.

'Hiya! Me again! Can I come back in?'

'No.'

'I said can I come back in again?' Increased dementia.

'No.'

'What?!'

'What do you want?'

'Can I come in for a minute?'

'I'm asleep.'

'Are you angry with me?'

'No I'm just asleep.'

'If you're angry then we need to discuss it!'

'I CAN'T HEAR YOU.'

She was annoyed with herself for reacting, and then almost instantly calm again, but she wasn't, couldn't, be angry with Mary-Marie. Because how could she be angry with someone of whom she had never had any expectation? Who was just a thing that happened? It was like being angry with the rain for raining, or shouting up at the heavens, fists raised, at an imaginary, vengeful creator. Mary-Marie continued to witter on the other side of the door until she became simply the dull buzzing of a white noise. Alice's mobile beeped. She ignored it, and instead turned inwards on herself, storing everything up, rediscovering a greatness. She closed her eyes again and soared a little higher. Freshness, lightness - and then ultimately still.

Shopping

'I'm really looking forward to meeting Lara!' said Mary-Marie.

They were sat too close on the number two four three bus. Mary-Marie was not meeting Lara. Alice was meeting Lara and Mary-Marie was going to do something else. Alone. They just happened to be on the same bus and Mary-Marie had managed to confuse herself. Alice was amazed by the extent to which she had managed to confuse herself. The bus approached Liverpool Street Station and Alice made a dash for the exit.

'I don't think you'll have time – '

Alice swung herself quickly out of the door – the bus was still moving – and tripped slightly on the curb. Mary-Marie tapped ominously at the window but the bus was going faster now and she'd been too slow off the mark.

(*Foiled!* thought Alice, as a comic book hero, and imagined Mary-Marie punching her palm with a fist.)

She could already see Lara, who was sucking up an iced Soya frappachino through a straw – it was the first week in a very hot August – and wearing shorts. The shorts were 80s' Nike. Orange and silky. She wore them with box fresh high-top 80s' style Nike trainers, a cut up t-shirt and matching sweat bands. It was very August 2003.

Alice ran up to her, a little giddy from the escape.

'I like your trainers,' she said breathlessly, and glanced over her shoulder just in case.

'Thanks. Limited edition. Got a contact in New York,' replied Lara.

'Can you get them over here yet?' Alice said.

'No,' said Lara. She finished her frappacino, threw the plastic cup on the ground and kicked it with a limited edition ease. Alice was impressed. Lara seemed especially trendy today. She wore trainers other people couldn't get and knew how to kick a coffee cup. Alice aspired gently in the heat.

'Lets get another coffee' said Lara, who might become excessively trendy at any moment, 'and then we'll do some shopping.'

They walked away from Liverpool Street Station, past the Starbucks and the market, and got another coffee in a glass walled coffee shop off Brick Lane. It was full of girls with dark fringes and a bit of 80s' Nike. There were stacks of magazines that they both flicked through. They analysed the other girls' styles in hushed tones, and the magazines in louder ones, and sipped their drinks. It'd been weeks since Camilla's party. They didn't want to offend anyone, but certain issues needed to be discussed. One girl's fringe was slightly too long.

'What are the styles like round Stoke Newington?' asked Lara.

'So, so. Posh hippies and yummy mummies mainly. A 'really laidback kinda vibe" said Alice. She made a knowingly geeky gesture to acknowledge the use of punctuation, and thought of two quite different men that she had known, though never in the biblical sense, then let it glide away without comment, as she sipped her coffee in the style of Anna Karina.

'I don't understand hippies in cities,' said Lara.

'No I don't. The city is for gloss and grime,' said Alice. She believed edge outweighed pretty, but that neither were mutually exclusive. Lara nodded in agreement. They shared similar priorities and wanted to confirm them.

'But then I don't understand why people would want to slow down or live in the countryside either,' rejoined Lara.

'No, I don't. It says you've given in,' said Alice who, when in London, England, didn't like to go beyond zone two.

Lara told Alice how she had been working for a magazine called *Tank*, and was considering re-locating to East Berlin. They sipped their coffee and certain issues were continually discussed.

'It's cheaper than here. And more accessible,' said Lara, but she was worried because she only spoke English.

There was a pause while they each thought about the implications of the language barrier, and came to different conclusions. The pause continued past the thought, more coffee was sipped.

'I do like your trainers,' said Alice for the second time, 'and I'm not normally a trainer person.'

'Do you think they're still fresh?' said Lara, who was worried that Hoxton was over. She had recently attended a party with an Electro Sucks theme. Someone had set fire to a Fishcherspooner record while people danced and cheered.

'I think they're fresh,' said Alice, 'they're making me re-assess my position on trainers. Even Camilla's reconsidering trainers.'

'I'd never have considered Camilla a trainer person,' said Lara with genuine surprise.

Lara told Alice how she had started getting her hair cut at Aveda, which only used organic products. That she had started having acupuncture. That she had broken up with her new boyfriend for an unspecified reason. That she had fallen out with Lucy.

'Lucy is a cunting mentalist,' said Lara without elaboration.

There was a tapping on the glass and both girls started. Alice, who had been leaning back in her chair, nearly fell off it. Mary-Marie had come up from nowhere and mouthed something through the window.

'What?' shouted Lara.

'If you're mad with me I think we should talk about it,' echoed faintly back.

Alice was still reeling. Fortunately all the seats in the café were taken. She wondered if she'd have to move house again. Women really did need occupations. Mary-Marie needed a baby or a disease to sap her energy she reflected, and drank some more of her coffee.

'Are you coming to *Return To New York*? It's this weekend.' said Lara. Return To New York was a club night at the Great Eastern Hotel. It was supposed to be very glamorous.

Alice wasn't sure. She hadn't been before. She should have been. It'd been cool for a while now, and Alice was cool. But then she was also sophisticated. Who else was going, and what would it be like?

'Armond maybe, and Camilla and Crispin and maybe some people from the magazine,' said Lara, 'it's always a good-looking crowd. Electroclash and tonnes of coke.'

It seemed inevitable then. Alice wondered what pretty shroud she'd wear as she danced and cheered and watched Rome fall. Lately she'd considered spending less on clothes. She thought about it for a while and drank some more of her coffee.

'I really like your shorts,' said Alice, 'and I wouldn't normally have said that I was into shorts.'

'Yeah the shorts *are* good' said Lara with something akin to relief. 'I'm less sure about the trainers, but the shorts are still fresh.'

They finished their coffees and walked down Brick Lane together and looked in all the shops. Alice had decided to buy some shorts herself. Perhaps not as overtly trendy as Lara's, but shorts all the same. There was a linen pair in Rokit that might be radically conservative. They had nice buttons. Maybe she would wear them to *Return to New York* at the weekend, which she had now decided to go to, as it was important to have an occupation. She touched the linen and thought about creases.

'Is it true about Krakow?' said Lara.

'What?'

'About it being the new East Berlin?'

'Oh I don't know,' said Alice, 'I just heard someone in a gallery say it and it sounded good. So then I said it.'

'I don't know if I could cut it in Krakow. It'd be really cold,' said Lara.

'I wouldn't mind that. Coldness and cruelty, black fur and white snow.'

'Not really my style,' said Lara, and pulled at the luminous corners of her shorts and laughed. Alice laughed too. Lara's style was fun-loving.

'At one point I had my heart set on living in Rome, but it wasn't meant to be,' said Alice.

'Rome's not very trendy,' said Lara.

'I know, but I thought it might be sophisticated.'

They were both looking at the same pair of gold pumps. They were very pretty. They also had an edge. They had tiny chocolate coloured butterflies embroidered on them with tiny amber stones sparkling on the tiny wings. Alice wriggled her foot inside a pump. They were nice. They fitted. She looked at Lara.

'It's ok you can buy them if you like,' she said.

'I don't mind if you buy them.' said Alice.

In the end neither of them bought them, though Alice bought the shorts. They walked down Brick Lane in the hot summer sun and discussed the styles. Lara was going to get a new haircut next week, she felt really dull and like everyone else with her hair and ready for a change, would Alice like to come with her and get her hair cut too? Alice decided that she would. Maybe they could get it done before *Return to New York*? Maybe they could both go to *Return to New York* together with their new haircuts and new shorts? Wouldn't that be nice? Yes it would.

'Would you like to go out with the Marquis de Sade?' asked Alice. Lara looked confused.

'I don't know. I'd have to meet him.'

It was a lovely afternoon. Somehow gracious.

Opera

The man beside her had paid for the tickets, the rest, when the seats were of a burgundy velvet upholstery, was incidental. Familiar in froufrou, lit with warm gold, she presented a coherent picture of dissipation. A small hand reached for the opera glasses, uncertain of their etiquette.

'Who wrote it again? Verdi?'

'Yes,' said her companion, a handsome smiling man.

'And what was his first name?'

'Giuseppe.'

'And was he an Italian?'

'Yes. Shhhh.'

(*I am intensely irritating*, thought Alice, and then: *he thinks he is going to get laid.*)

She reached for, and then held the opera glasses, her nails were coloured a subtle peach, and the curtains drew back on social scandal:

Violetta, a famous tart, was giving a party. She wore a massive ebony satin dress, spangled more lovely than a fictional night sky, with a thousand starry diamonds. Her hair, which was jet-black and possibly a wig, sat in tight, glossy ringlets across her large pale face, soon to be moist with exertion. Her blue eyes looked out imploringly towards the crowd and, sometimes, when she held a long note for a long time, the loose flesh under her chin trembled.

The whole stage joined in. Songs were sung to the pleasures of wine. More excessive costumes glinted in more excessive lighting. Violetta laughed and danced and charmed her way across the room, swooshed past many a well-groomed and singing admirer, in a confident tremble of further song. Her hair and dress and skin became one big cream cake of luscious luxury, glinting beneath *six* (three painted, three real) chandeliers. Too much, never enough, and arching over, upwards, and away.

Alice was pleased they hadn't tried to go all modern. There were big frocks and bigger hair throughout. A glitzy reproduction of 1850s Paris consummate with a fashionable hint of corruption. She sighed in ecstasy, and this was shortly followed by an aria to longing.

'And did Giuseppe Verdi come up with the story?' She enjoyed using the full name now she knew it.

'No it was originally *La Dame aux Camelias* by someone French.'

'And who was that?'

'What?'

'The French man who wrote *La Dame aux Camelias*, who was he?'

'I don't know. Shhhh.' He pressed a finger against his tolerant, well-read mouth, and Alice, as an obedient child, turned her attention back towards the glinting, shimmering, one hundred and twenty pound a ticket, marvel.

> Violetta was so beautiful and not as fat as one had expected. Things changed, and she and Alfredo had moved to a house in the country. There were hints of illness and something about a wilted flower. Despite a lot of singing, there didn't seem to be many proper songs.

Notwithstanding this Alice knew that she liked the Opera, and that this she had always known. Her mind wandered and was drawn back in like a long sweep of the cello bow. There was going to be a beginning, a middle and an end and all based around a proper theme. The Opera presented itself, through both cost and education, as not for everyone, and yet it wasn't a medium that asked for concentration, just an indolent, informed voyeurism. *It is perfection,* thought Alice, and a finger softly touched a frill.

> Somewhere amidst the lavish and ongoing spectacle Violetta renounced Alfredo. His father arrived and persuaded her that it was a bad idea. Violetta is a famous tart, his son comes from a good family, and everyone's reputations will be ruined, unhappiness for everyone, etc. So be a clever girl, he urges in Italian verse, because it all makes sense.
>
> It being a pure and noble love, Violetta complies with his request, selflessly prizing her lover's greater good above her own.
>
> She leaves. There is heartache. Then an interval.

They have two drinks set aside in the bar. Alice didn't realise you could do this at the Opera. Order your drinks beforehand, and then collect them half way through without queuing. It is a night where so many new things offer themselves up for her delight, and where she accepts without hesitation. Alice sips a Martin. In a Martini glass. And crosses her legs so as to make the frills rustle and show her lovely, lovely legs.

'Did you like the singing?'

'In places. But I loved the Opera.'

'The soprano is world renowned.'

Do people really have these conversations? They must do. She was really having one. Boredom on a patrician level – it signified a new phase in life. Or maybe she wasn't even bored, and boredom was a habit. She had loved the Opera, and especially the soprano's ebony dress.

'I think the costumes are good. Do you know who designed the costumes?'

'No.'

'It reminds me of that film, *Moulin Rouge*, have you seen it?'

'What?'

'Moulin Rouge. It's a film with Nicole Kidman and Ewan McGregor. It's ok, the costumes are nice – '

'Yes I've seen it. It's based on *La Traviata*.'

He looks so upset that Alice re-crosses and re-rustles and gives in and gives a little. She knows she is being irritating, that money and expectation sits between them, that she invited them in and is therefore indebted.

'The aria was superb,' she says, and he looks so relieved it stabs her. He smiles at Alice and Alice smiles back. He is very handsome but a bit sexless. They sit that way a while. Alice drains her glass and a bell rings. They return to their seats.

> More richly furnished rooms. More suffering. Violetta lies pale and helpless – a fallen woman, Fragonard's temptation of Eve eighty years on – and coughs up blood. She is dying of consumption. A letter arrives. Alfredo will return. He has found out about what went on between her and his father, but he doesn't care about reputations, only his equally pure and noble love for Violetta! Alfredo returns. Violetta hands him a portrait to remind him of the woman who loved him so much (*Prendi, quest e l'immagine!*). Then her diseased lungs fail her and she dies. Rapturous applause. The End.

Alice sips on a second Martini. It is only manners considering. Rustle and cross. Cross, cross rustle. Alice sips on a second Martini.

'I was moved,' says Alice, who has neither cried nor fainted. 'It was different to how I expected, but I'll never forget the wonderful stage design.'

'Right.'

He is disappointed. Alice realises not only that she is failing to live up to her image, but also that she might be being deliberately unkind. She hadn't realised this was something she was capable of. She feels that she is lacking an adequate means of compensation for her deficiency in appropriate responses, but reasons that as that's how it is, that's how it can only be, and through this simple chain of thought the guilt begins to dissolve. It's not as if she even asked for the ticket. And then all the guilt is gone. Alice doesn't give much, but she doesn't expect *anything*. She sips on a second Martini, not essentially with pleasure, but with acceptance. She has deliberately chosen an expensive drink and consumes it with an approach that is Zen. She drinks a drink that tastes the same as other drinks, and slowly heat rises.

'And the costumes. But I think I already said that.'

'Yes.'

'And the love and death and death of love, that's always a sure fire winner for me.'

'Umm.' He shuffles. A rustle. A cross cross shuffle rustle. An abstract arrangement that doesn't encourage dancers. Lately she has been trying to listen to John Cage, Philip Glass and other minimalist composers, but, being a cunt for a key change, still isn't sure if this is really her style. She holds a pink ruffle between her thumb and forefinger and looks at her new male friend. Alice smiles at him, and he smiles at Alice. She lowers her eyelids, then looks up through the lashes:

'I don't,' she says 'really know much about the Opera. But I know what I like.'

1- Dark chocolate with cherries.
2- A second-hand china cat.
3- Jean Paul Belmondo.
4- The smell of French vanilla.

She drains her glass and laughs. She has had two Martinis but she feels very, very high. It is cold in the bar and people are beginning to leave. Alice shivers and pulls a white mink stole around her shoulders. A large faux-diamond ring glints as it catches the light. She is flushed from the alcohol. Pink cheeks, white fur and summer twilight. And suddenly Alice remembers a small part of a long sentence. She turns to her companion:

'Si... il m' était laissé assez longtemps.'

But she only has a little, and so, impulsively, she kisses him. He kisses her back and they stand that way for over a minute in a crush of frills and his lambs-wool jumper and some stubble and some loose hair. His tongue in her frigid mouth, and her head back a little. And then it passes. And off, and alone, and into the summer night.

Intermission

'I can't believe you've actually got a job,' said Armond. 'It's appalling. I mean actually *trying* for things. It lacks dignity.'

Saturday. Rock oysters and dry white in Soho in summer. British men kissing foreign men, and meals eaten out of doors.

'I don't think I did try. I was just broke. It's a case of tactical necessity.'

'Give me one good thing about it.'

'I have my own torch.'

'Like Florence Nightingale?' It was rhetorical.

The lady of the lamp added lemon to her oyster and thought about zinc levels, anti-oxidants, omega three oils – a zealot at heart. They were all into health at the moment which was convenient. Camilla had developed a wheat allergy. Lara got her hair cut at Aveda, where they only used organic products. And Alice Grisham added lemon to her oyster and thought about zinc levels.

'I can't decide about your hair either. Is it actually any good?'

'Yes actually, it's very good.'

Shorter, softer, something modernist to frame the face was needed now. It was the second week in a hot September, five days ago she had turned twenty-four and was now prepared for a new kind of fun.

'I mean Alice, you're *almost* verging on radical. But the shorts are... better.'

'Yes, the shorts are the best.'

And there was real glee at her choice of shorts – which were high-waisted, vintage, linen Yves Saint Laurent, off-white with side-tie detail and button-down back pockets – buttons that were real tortoiseshell! They were the shorts to take you places and to go places in. In a photo-shoot on the Nile with palms and leopards. Hiding behind over-large sunglasses while hanging out in Saint Tropez – but she was twenty-four now and these thoughts must always be delivered with a very wry smile and even then a risk.

Armond added lemon to his oyster. He was planning to cut down on the crack, he had paid to join a gym, and it was he who had told Alice about the importance of zinc to the immune system.

'Actually my shirt's the best. It's Prada' he says.

Which is the Italian for self-respect. Which is the in-joke for a man in touch with his own bloody-nosed mortality bitching at his fag-hag friend. Armond stares into the back of a knife and gently pulls at a crease by his eye. He's just so tired all the time. And then there's this constant pain in the chest...

'Do you think it's worse,' says Alice, 'to be a spinster or a gay?'

Soho in summer. Foreign men held hands with British men in tight t-shirts and denim cut-offs, coffee and beer were drunk out of doors, Essex boys and their girls out for a day's shopping in the West End, tourists buying all manner of shit emblazoned with large breasts and the union jack. Armond orders another bottle, and Alice sits silently, feeling the heat on her neck, and the wet backs of her knees pressed firmly against the warm leatherette seating. She waves the menu absently to and fro creating a breeze against her damp forehead. *Mother*, she thinks, caught off guard by the action, *I am turning into my mother*.

Across the street two Spanish boys argue loudly. One pushes the other. Screams at him, slaps his face. Alice looks on, vaguely impressed by the emotion, and wonders whether the linen creases are noticeable in her new shorts.

'Are you worried about your shorts?'

They both watch the slapped man burst into tears. He shouts something incomprehensible in Spanish and storms off. In the commotion he has spilt coffee down the front of his white jeans, the crotch of which are now beige. The slapping man's face contorts with grief. He runs after the other, grabs his arm, crying too now, asking him to stay. They stand on the corner bickering. The first man points to the coffee stain. Shakes his head. The second man puts his hands on his shoulders, shakes him slightly, smiles nervously, hopefully, scans the other man's face in search of laughter and acquittal.

Alice tops her glass up and squints into the sun. The wine is very dry. She adds a little water to it, and then puts a piece of lemon in the glass. Then she realises what she's done and removes the lemon. Her fingers are wet so she wipes them on her shorts. Now her shorts are wet, so she dabs them with a napkin. Finally she sips her drink while Armond watches with a sideways look. He is laughing slightly. Alice laughs too.

'Have you ever had a broken heart?' she asks.

'Well, you know, I'm a creative individual so four or five times a day.'

'Sometimes I think I was born with one.'

'You were born looking out the window.'

And walking in the rain with her collar turned up. Listening to The Smiths and painting it black. You were one type or the other – it was not a thing to be attributed a specific cause. But it is hard to be sad in the summer, and a man with a pleasant face smiles at Alice and Alice thinks, *next time I will smile back.*

'I'm thinking of applying for an MA,' says Alice. 'It'll give me more options.' By this she means it'll give her less options and take back the responsibility for a while. She has done the research. There are several London colleges she could apply to. Some do a one-year course, others a two. One does a three-year course and at present this is the most appealing. Her hair is hot and heavy. It smells of camomile.

'I was thinking of doing the same,' says Armond, 'the boredom is literally killing me. I thought about doing some charity work, but then I don't want to feel guilty when I let them down.'

The Spanish boys hug awkwardly and begin to laugh, and walk down the road together. The boy who did the slapping slips his hand in the other boy's back pocket. They carry on walking.

Alice and Armond discuss Rimbaud. By his early twenties he had given up poetry and become a gunrunner in Africa. The continual derangement had only lasted so long, and then a new reality took hold. It was possible to experience life after art. It was possible to see new things. And these possibilities remained just that.

The street stank in a midday glare and Alice thought: *even the sun is disgusting.*

Printed in the United Kingdom
by Lightning Source UK Ltd.
123601UK00001B/13-39/A